A Pickpocket's Tale

KAREN SCHWABACH

A Pickpocket's Tale

RANDOM HOUSE 🏠 NEW YORK

Copyright © 2006 by Karen Schwabach
Jacket illustration copyright © 2006 by Dan Craig

All rights reserved. Published in the United States by Random House Children's Books,
a division of Random House, Inc., New York.

RANDOM HOUSE and colophon are registered trademarks of Random House, Inc.

www.randomhouse.com/kids

Educators and librarians, for a variety of teaching tools, visit us at
www.randomhouse.com/teachers

Library of Congress Cataloging-in-Publication Data
Schwabach, Karen.
A pickpocket's tale / Karen Schwabach.
p. cm.
SUMMARY: When Molly, a ten-year-old orphan, is arrested for picking pockets
in London in 1731, she is banished to America and serves as an indentured servant
for a New York City family that expects her to follow their Jewish traditions.
ISBN-13: 978-0-375-83379-3 (trade) — ISBN-13: 978-0-375-93379-0 (lib. bdg.)
ISBN-10: 0-375-83379-X (trade) — ISBN-10: 0-375-93379-4 (lib. bdg.)
[1. Pickpockets—Fiction. 2. Indentured servants—Fiction. 3. Judaism—Customs and practices—
Fiction. 4. Slavery—Fiction. 5. Jews—New York (state)—New York—Fiction. 6. Orphans—
Fiction. 7. New York (N.Y.)—History—Colonial period, ca. 1600-1775—Fiction.] I. Title.
PZ7.S3988Pic 2006 [Fic]—dc22 2005024091

Printed in the United States of America 10 9 8 7 6 5 4 3 2 1

First Edition

With love to Gommy

Dear Reader,

Some characters in this book speak an old London dialect called Flash or Flash-cant. Thieves invented this secret language so that they could hide what they were saying. If you have trouble understanding the characters speaking Flash-cant, turn to the glossary on page 219.

Karen Schwabach

A Pickpocket's Tale

One

"**The law is!**" The judge adjusted the black velvet cap atop his full-bottomed white wig and gazed down at the manacled prisoner before him in the cobbled court of Sessions House Yard. He looked around at the other chained prisoners waiting in the cold, open yard, then over at the dismal huddle of people whom he had already sentenced.

He pursed his lips and continued. "That you shall return from here, to the place whence you came. And from there to the Place of Execution. Where you shall hang by the neck until the body be dead! Dead! Dead! And the Lord have mercy on your soul."

The prisoner gasped and turned white. He stumbled backward, stricken. The judge smiled in grim satisfaction while the bailiffs dragged the prisoner off to a corner to join the others who had been condemned.

Molly shifted from one aching foot to the other, trying to ease the weight of the chains on her ankles. It was the fourth death sentence she had heard that morning, Molly thought, or maybe the fifth. It wasn't getting any easier to guess what the judge was going to say when her turn came. Everyone knew that you could be hanged for stealing anything worth more than a shilling, in London in this year 1730. Even if it was your first offense. Or you could steal more than that, a dozen times, and live. And it didn't seem to matter if you were only ten years old, like Molly, or really old . . . forty, even. There was no way of telling how it worked.

You couldn't tell bleedin' much from the judge's speeches either, Molly thought. He sat there like a great, gloating carrion crow, looking down at the prisoners from his high perch. He talked a lot of bleedin' rubbish about their sins, and the great wisdom and mercy of the law, and the love of the King for his subjects, and he said that some sins (like stealing a knife or a ring) were too great to be forgiven on earth. And while he talked, he fingered the black velvet cap that he would put on for death sentences and turned it slowly in his hands, looking from the cap to the prisoner and from the prisoner to the cap. There was no way you could tell whether he was going to say the cramping-words—the death sentence—or something else until he either clapped the black hat on his head or else set it gently down among the piles of flowers on the high bench before him.

Today was a sentencing day. The prisoners had already been found guilty. They had been waiting in the yard since before the first dim rays of the December dawn melted the frost on the cobbles. Molly longed for something to eat. Something to eat, and something warm on her hands and feet. Some of the prisoners had stuffed straw into their shoes to keep out the cold, but Molly's wood-and-leather clogs didn't have any room for straw in them. They were too small as it was. Molly had grown in the months she'd been in prison. Her skinny wrists stuck out from her sleeves, and the hem of her linsey-woolsey dress and the shift underneath hung almost two inches above her ankles, showing the too-big gray woolen stockings that had been her mother's. She caught sight of her reflection in a puddle at her feet. Dark brown eyes stared out of a thin, pale face. Her tangled black hair just reached her shoulders. It had been longer once, but she had cut it off two years ago when she'd had the smallpox.

Molly looked up at the other chained prisoners near her and tried to guess something about her fate from them. It seemed like the bailiffs and turnkeys were herding together people who were going to get the same sentences. Well, One-Eyed Jake was near her. He was a flash-cove on the rattling lay, stealing from coaches. Molly had seen him do it—sneaking among coaches that were stuck in the mass of vehicles crammed together, trying to get through the narrow city gates. He would quietly slice through the leather top of a carriage and take whatever he could find inside.

Then there was another kinchin mort like herself. Molly stiffened as she recognized Hesper Crudge. Molly had never spoken to Hesper, but she knew who Hesper was. Everyone did. At least everyone on the canting lay—all the thieves of London. Hesper had a reputation for blowing the gab. If you reported someone for stealing and they were hanged, you got a reward of forty pounds. Or so the law said. Molly had never heard of anyone actually getting the forty pounds, but Hesper was willing to keep trying.

She was about Molly's age but a little taller, with hair that might be blond under the dirt. She had the narrow, knowing eyes of an old criminal, and a cutthroat's face, carefully schooled to show no expression. When Hesper saw Molly looking at her, she sneered and spat on the ground.

And who was this old biddy on Molly's other side? She was ancient, at least thirty years old, her stringy hair graying and her sallow skin deeply scarred by smallpox. Molly had seen her around Bartholomew's Fair, selling handkerchiefs that weren't her own. That old woman looked very likely to be fruit for the Deadly Nevergreen Tree, as they called the gallows at Tyburn.

The woman looked at Molly and smiled reassuringly.

Over in the corner, a bailiff was stirring the coals to

keep the branding iron hot. Was someone going to be branded soon, or was he just making sure the fire stayed lit? Molly could smell the coal smoke from where she stood, but she couldn't feel the heat. It would be nice to get close enough to that fire to warm her aching fingers and toes. But not too close. Molly felt dizzy with cold, and with hunger. She hadn't eaten since the day before yesterday.

A gentleman was making his way across the yard, a nib cull who clearly didn't belong in the Old Bailey. He was dressed in pearl-gray velvet knee breeches and a matching velvet coat. Molly wondered what he was doing here. He stopped a bailiff and began talking to him, gesturing once in Molly's direction. She thought she had seen him somewhere before.

"Oyez! Oyez!" The bailiffs were suddenly hustling them forward, Molly and the clutch of prisoners around her—Hesper Crudge and One-Eyed Jake and the ancient mort with the gallows face. It was too sudden. Molly wasn't ready. She panicked, looked around wildly, her heart thumping.

The ancient mort met her eyes. "Chin up, ducks." She touched Molly's shoulder gently, her chains clanking. "It's soon over."

"Silence!" roared a bailiff.

Molly shrugged the old woman's hand away. It *wasn't* soon over. Molly had seen hangings. Plenty of them.

The judge was looking at them now, fingering the black velvet cap. He looked at One-Eyed Jake, and then at Hesper. "His Majesty is always concerned about the happiness and well-being of his subjects," he said.

He twirled the black cap thoughtfully in his hands. Molly felt her stomach sink.

"His Majesty naturally wishes that all of his subjects could be happy together, enjoying the magnificent bounty of his generous rule." He looked meaningfully at Molly. Molly looked away, unable to meet his burning eyes.

"However!"

The judge looked at them. They all looked away. Molly felt the ancient mort touch her shoulder again. This time Molly let her; she felt helpless, like a twig caught in the rushing current under London Bridge.

"It is necessary, for the happiness and peace of the realm, that some of his subjects be taken out of it! Therefore . . ."

Molly felt her mouth grow dry. She was no longer aware of hunger or the cold in her hands and feet. Her legs felt weak and rubbery.

The judge looked at the black cap. He turned it over, ready to put it on his head. He admired the lining for a moment. Then he looked up again.

"The law is!"

He looked at them. They looked at him. It was an

awful moment, a frozen moment that seemed to stretch on for centuries.

"That you shall return to the place from whence you came. And from there be transported to His Majesty's colony in Virginia. There to remain for a period of seven years." He set the black cap down.

And Molly fainted.

Two

When Molly came around, she was back in Newgate Prison. The smell assaulted her before she opened her eyes. It was a stench of unwashed clothes and bodies, of rotting straw and waste, of bad liquor and bad teeth and the seeping miasma of jail fever and death.

She was in the Hold, the underground dungeon assigned to sentenced prisoners who had no money to pay for a cell above ground. Someone must have carried her here. A prisoner, or a bailiff? Would she have to pay them for it? You had to pay for everything in Newgate: your food, your cell, everything. Even your chains—if you could pay to have your chains removed, the turnkeys took them off. Otherwise they left them on.

Molly sat up on the cold, damp floor. Something crackled under her. At first she thought it was straw, but when she took up a handful, she found it was insects.

Dead insects. Heaps of them, centuries of them—enough to cover the floor, like straw or sand.

She scrambled to her feet, brushing frantically at her skirts and hair.

"There, love." The old woman from Sessions House Yard was at her side. "Don't think about it and it's no different from having straw underneath. Feeling any better?"

"Uh." Molly felt sick, and her head hurt. And she didn't like that this woman was still hanging around her. What did the old mort want?

"We were lucky, mind. It could have been much worse. And America may not be as bad as they say." The mort shook her head. "I thought I was for it, to tell the truth. This was my second offense."

Molly was interested in spite of herself. "What did you do?"

"I didn't do anything," said the woman. "But I was caught with a piece of velvet cloth worth fifteen pounds."

"Fifteen pounds!" Molly tried not to sound impressed. She'd never stolen anything worth that much.

"I was just holding it for a friend." The woman looked at Molly curiously. "And what did you do, a little scrapper like you?"

Molly looked her in the eyes. "Nothing."

The woman laughed. "Of course. None of us did nothing." She put an arm around Molly's shoulder. "What's your name, child?"

"Molly," she said, edging away.

"Just Molly? All by itself?"

"Molly Abraham."

"I'm Elizabeth Wilkes. I have a little girl about your age."

"Elizabeth Wilkes? Ha! Her name's Liftin' Lizzie," someone muttered from the floor.

Mrs. Wilkes was about to respond with her foot when the door creaked open and one of the turnkeys came in, holding a burning torch and leading two well-dressed, clean-looking gentlemen. In the light of the torch, Molly could see that one of them was the gentleman in pearl-gray velvet who had pointed to her in Sessions House Yard.

The gentleman in gray wrinkled up his nose. He looked quite ill from the smell of the Hold. Well, what did he expect, a nib cull like him coming into a plaguey hole like this? Served him right to be sick.

"I suppose the mort, er, girl, you're looking for is in here," said the turnkey. "I couldn't say which one she is, though. Don't you know what she looks like?"

Several women gathered around the gentlemen, jostling them. "Are you looking for me, ducks?" one of them asked.

The turnkey pushed the woman aside without

looking at her. "The gentlemen are looking for a Jewess," he said.

"A very young woman," said the cull in gray velvet. Molly was almost sure she'd seen him before today. Had she picked his pocket once?

"Girl," said his companion. "The Jewish girl that was sentenced today."

"Oh, I know!" Mrs. Wilkes stepped into the torch-light. "That'll be her over here, then. Won't the gennel-mun step this way?" She tried to curtsey, and stumbled. Molly wondered if Mrs. Wilkes was drunk.

The turnkey and the gentlemen moved forward through the gloom. Molly watched them pick their way distastefully over the prone figures of sleeping prisoners till they were standing before her. The turnkey held the torch over Molly, and the gentlemen gazed at her thoughtfully.

"This is a sorry place to find a daughter of Israel," said the man in gray velvet.

"Huh?" said Molly. She noted with interest that Mrs. Wilkes was going through the two gentlemen's pockets. They didn't seem to feel a thing.

"I said," repeated the gentleman, "that this is a sorry place to find a daughter of Israel. I am Mr. Israel Men-dez, and this gentleman here is my business partner, Mr. Lopez."

"What makes you think I'm your daughter?" said Molly suspiciously. She watched Mrs. Wilkes extract a watch from the gray velvet coat and feel for the catch to release it.

"Not my daughter," said Mr. Mendez. "A daughter of Israel. A Jewess. I said that it's unfortunate to find a Jewess who has not only abandoned the law, but has sunk to such depths as this."

"Oh." Molly shrugged, watched Mrs. Wilkes free Mr. Mendez's watch from its chain and slip it silently into the folds of her woolen shift. "Well, I can't see that it's any of your bleedin' business."

Mr. Mendez turned a dull angry red in the torch-light. "It is always our business to watch out for each other, as you would have known if you had had any kind of teaching. I take it your mother is no longer with us?"

"She's . . . yes," said Molly. She didn't want to think about her mother, and she didn't like this cove who was asking her nosy questions and looking at her as if she were a disease. "I mean, she's not."

"I understand you have been sentenced to transportation. I shall be corresponding with our people in America to alert them to the situation. Meanwhile . . ." He looked at Molly and then at the turnkey. Molly wished he wouldn't speak such nib lingo. She had no idea what he was talking about, and she didn't trust him. "How much to remove the chains?" he asked the turnkey.

"Fifteen shillings," said the turnkey with a smirk.

"And to feed her until she's transported?"

"Three shillings sixpence a week, plus two for beer, plus four for garnish."

"Garnish?" asked Mr. Mendez.

"I'm Garnish," explained the turnkey.

"Very well, we want her fed and we want the chains off. And we'll pay whatever ridiculous fee you charge to get her out of this charnel house into a real cell with a window. Now, are there any other Jews in this wretched hole?"

"Not that I know of, sir," said the turnkey. "But if Your Honor chooses to look above stairs?"

As they turned to go, Mr. Mendez's companion, Mr. Lopez, turned back and rested his hand for a moment on Molly's head. "There, take courage, child," he said. "God will watch over you. And there's for you."

He put something round and heavy into her hands. Molly lifted it to her face and saw and smelled that it was a whole, real orange.

Molly hoped the money for her food and to have her chains off hadn't been slipped out of Mr. Mendez's velvet coat into Mrs. Wilkes's pocket. Apparently it hadn't, because the next day she was taken out of the Hold to a ward above ground, where a little light and air came through from a high window. The fresh air didn't make much difference—the stench of rot and failure were as much a part of the prison walls as the stones themselves. Newgate had been a prison for more than five hundred years.

There were ten other prisoners in the cell, men and women, and no furniture except straw on the floor, which at least was better than the dead bugs in the Hold. But any kind of cell at all was expensive at Newgate, and Molly suspected Mr. Mendez must have spent a small fortune. Her chains were taken off. And twice a day after that—twice a day, not just once—she was allowed to go to the taproom for a beaker of beer, a bowl of pease porridge, and a hunk of black bread to dip in it.

She was glad to have these things. But she didn't see what nib culls like Mr. Mendez and Mr. Lopez had to do with her. She knew she was Jewish, because her mother had said so once or twice. Angrily, not as if it were something she liked. And then, before Mama died, she'd told Molly to go to the synagogue in Bevis Marks, that the other Jews would help her.

Suddenly Molly smiled. She knew where she had seen Mr. Mendez before! He'd come to see Mama once, in their room in the house with the smashed staircase in Cucumber Alley, off Seven Dials. Why had he come? Molly was sure he hadn't been one of Mama's men friends. She remembered he'd talked to Mama in his scolding way, probably the same stuff about the law and being a sorry excuse for a daughter of Israel he'd said to Molly. Mama had leapt up and seized a kitchen knife, and she went for him like a madwoman. Mama wouldn't have actually hurt him—probably—but Mr.

Mendez hadn't known that. Molly smiled at the memory of Mr. Mendez running out of the room and crashing to the story below as he missed the stairs that weren't there.

It had been brave of him to come at all. Molly wondered if he knew how brave. Nib culls in velvet clothes who ventured into the London slums didn't always come out alive. Only ragged, thinly clad folk like Molly could slip through the alleys in relative safety.

After Mama died, Molly had ignored her instructions to go looking for other Jews. She didn't need their help. She knew how to survive in London, how to pick pockets and sell what she got. But now she was being transported, sent to a place called Virginia that was so awful that going there was almost as bad as being hanged. And the other Jews knew all about it, and they weren't doing a thing to stop it. It was nice to have the food and to have her chains off, but she didn't think that Mr. Mendez had been much help in the long run.

Three

16　**The ship was** called the *Good Intention*, and Molly hated it on sight. She hated the way it rocked precariously in the gentle lapping of the waters of the Pool of London, and she hated the dizzying sway of the three masts when she looked up at them. The yardarms that crossed the masts and the forest of ropes and rigging that hung from them looked like the bones of a great, stark skeleton. Or a gallows. The ship beneath it all seemed small and pitiful, a brown pile of wet, rotten-looking wood.

When Molly went inside, down in the hold, she hated it even more.

The hold was dark, and smelled of dead fish and spoiled meat. Two lonely beams of sunlight came from portholes set high in the bulkhead. The sloping deck rocked slightly beneath Molly's feet. She heard the other prisoners stumbling about, bumping into each other and cursing. As her eyes adjusted to the gloom, she gradually saw the people she had come on board with—a hundred men, women, and children. Mrs. Wilkes was standing near her. Molly hadn't seen the old mort since Mr. Mendez had paid for Molly's cell months ago. She didn't see One-Eyed Jake anywhere, though. Perhaps he had bribed his way out of Newgate, or died of jail fever.

"Scared, ain't you?" said a soft, insinuating voice.

Molly turned quickly. Hesper Crudge was standing an arm's length behind her, hands on her hips, bare feet apart, an evil grin on her cutthroat's face. They stared at each other. Like Molly, Hesper was small for her age, with the wiry, underfed build of the London streets. There was a look in her eyes that Molly had seen many times before: the calculating expression of someone who would do anything to anyone if she saw a way to gain from it, or even if she didn't.

"I'm never scared," said Molly.

"You were scared at the Old Bailey, weren't you? Scared of the nubbing-cheat. Fainted, didn't you? Like a fine lady." Hesper stretched out the last two words to make them more insulting.

"Stow your widdes!" said Molly angrily.

Hesper pushed Molly down onto the deck. She landed on a body that squirmed in protest. Molly stumbled to her feet again and pushed Hesper.

Hesper took a step backward but didn't fall.

Molly grabbed a handful of Hesper's dirty blond

hair and pulled. Hesper clawed at Molly's face with grubby broken fingernails. Molly closed her eyes tightly and butted her head into Hesper's stomach. They both fell on the deck and rolled into a cold, moldy-smelling puddle of bilgewater.

"Fight! Fight!" someone shouted.

"Threepence on the littler one!" That meant Molly.

"Ah, shut up. You don't have threepence."

Hesper was pulling Molly's hair so hard that Molly felt as if her head were being ripped apart. She buried her hands in Hesper's hair and pulled for all she was worth.

Then someone was grabbing her arms, prying her fingers loose, pulling her away.

"That's enough o' that!" It was Mrs. Wilkes. "We'll be at sea two months and more, and at this rate you'll kill each other before we make Gravesend."

Molly touched her stinging scalp. It hurt so much that she felt it must be bleeding, but it was dry to the touch. She fought back tears. Hesper wasn't going to make her cry. She sat down on the deck.

Hesper stood looking down at her, smirking to show that Molly hadn't hurt her at all.

"My name's Hesper Crudge," she said. As if Molly didn't know who Hesper was. Everyone did.

"That's your problem," said Molly.

"I've sent ten people to America already. On my evidence. People from my gang, people that trusted me. If

I don't like someone, I turn 'em in. It doesn't pay to get on my bad side."

"Then they'll all be waiting for you when we get there, won't they?" said Molly.

Hesper scowled. She hadn't thought of this before. Then the smirk was back. "Give me them stockings."

Molly folded her legs under her. "No."

"Give 'em to me. I want 'em." She reached toward Molly.

Mrs. Wilkes was suddenly there again, her arm around Molly's shoulders. "Leave off now. You leave her alone."

Hesper backed away slightly and shrugged. "Well, I don't care. I'll have those stockings when I want 'em. She has to sleep sometime." She slithered off into the murky darkness.

Mrs. Wilkes patted Molly's shoulder. "Never mind, love. You stay by me and that baggage won't have the clothes off you."

"But Liftin' Lizzie might take a fancy to them stockings," said someone in the darkness.

Mrs. Wilkes ignored that. "Do you have any money, Molly?"

"No," said Molly, stiffening and pulling away.

"You'd better give me your money if you have any. For safekeeping."

Somebody snorted in the darkness. "Safekeeping? Ha!"

"Well, it's up to you, love. But if I were you, I wouldn't want to keep my money about me." She patted Molly on the shoulder again. "There are some dangerous coves down here with us."

"I don't have any money," said Molly curtly. She had spent all she had on stale bread and weak ale during her first week in Newgate, long before her trial. She had nothing left worth stealing, but was surrounded by people who wanted to steal it.

None of the prisoners had been to Virginia before, but some of them knew people who had.

"Old Joey Truepenny," said a man chained to the far bulkhead. "You remember him? Sentenced to Virginia twice."

"Othello, you mean," said a woman near Molly, her voice carrying across the hold. "Cove who lived up on Pissing Lane by St. John's Gate? We called him Othello. Hanged, didn't he? Did he make a brave show of it?"

"He never did," said the man. "Second time, the judge gave him a choice, Virginia or the gallows, and he chose the gallows."

"Many do," said someone near him gloomily. "At least the nubbing-cheat is quick."

"Quicker, anyway. But old Joey, he told the judge he'd take the nubbing-cheat, and then he escaped by climbing through the roof of the . . ." The man's voice trailed off. The heavy hatch overhead had grated open, sending a blinding beam of sunlight into the dark hold.

Four men came thumping down the ladder—a velvet-coated sea captain, two muscular seamen, and a man with a quill pen and a little leather-bound book. The captain carried a stout wooden cudgel, which he brought down on the deck with a mighty smack.

"I'm Darby Mattock, and I am the master of this ship," said the captain, looking them over grimly. "That means after we stand out from Gravesend, I am the law. Any trouble from any of you and you go over the side and feed the sharks. Understand? When we reach America, all anyone'll know is that you died at sea. Which ain't a rare occurrence."

He thumped the cudgel again for emphasis. "Now, I have laid on fatback, hardtack, and grog for fourteen weeks' crossing. That's allowing one beaker of grog per prisoner per day. If you want more than that, you'll drink water."

There were grumbles of angry protest, and somebody called, "What about gin?" No sensible Londoners ever drank water if they could help it. Water was stinking, slimy stuff. Captain Mattock smashed the cudgel down on the deck again. There was silence.

"If we don't cross in fourteen weeks' time, you'll get hungry. Now, if anybody has any money, you might as well give it to me now."

There was silence for a moment; the prisoners waited.

Captain Mattock waited a moment too. Then he explained, "For ten shillings down, you get a beaker of beer a day. For ten shillings more, you get lemons against the scurvy. For a pound, you can have a pallet to lie on, and a blanket."

"If I had that kind of money, I wouldn't be here," someone muttered.

"Wished I'd've kept the eight pounds I paid to get me out of this," someone else said. "What a waste of money! You can't even pay an honest bribe no more."

Molly scowled. One beaker of grog a day! She was used to beer. Grog was water with a little rum added to make it safe for drinking. Molly hated grog. The way it burned her throat going down felt like drinking poison.

A man at the other end of the hold stood up, his chains clanking, and said, "A word, Master Mattock!"

The captain gestured him forward with his cudgel, and the man whispered in his ear. The captain nodded, looking interested.

"Very well. Anybody else have any money?"

Reluctantly, a few hands went up. The captain nodded to his clerk, who picked his way around the hold, pocketing coins and making notes in his book.

"What happens to us when we get to America?" someone asked.

"You'll be sold to pay for your passage, of course," said Captain Mattock.

"I'm not a prisoner," said another voice from the darkness. "I'm not supposed to be down here with all these prisoners."

"You have money to pay for your passage?" the captain asked sarcastically.

"No. I'm going as a servant. On an indenture."

"Well, then, you're a prisoner as far as I'm concerned." The captain nodded to his assistants and started up the ladder. The prisoner who had whispered to him went with them.

"Lucky cove," said Mrs. Wilkes. "He must've had enough money to buy himself."

"Well, I sure didn't find it last night when he was sleeping," a man said. A few people chuckled.

That evening there was a great creaking of ropes amid the masts and rigging. Captain Mattock's voice rang out in commands punctuated by frequent thumps of the cudgel on the deck. Now and then, the cudgel seemed to hit something softer, followed by gasps and groans. The ship finally began to move down the Thames toward Gravesend and the sea.

The male prisoners were brought up only once a day to walk around the deck, their chains dragging and clanking dismally on the salt-soaked boards. But the women and girls weren't chained, and were allowed up on deck whenever they wanted. Captain Mattock didn't consider them dangerous. Molly went up there often to breathe the clean, salty air away from the close, stinking hold. But the deck made her nervous. The sky was a great dome overhead that stretched farther than she could see in any direction, and there was nothing at her back no matter which way she turned.

For the first few days, land was always visible on the horizon, and Molly kept hoping that the ship would turn around and go back to it. After all, something could go wrong, Captain Mattock could discover a problem with the ship and return for repairs, or even cancel the voyage.

If he did, Molly thought, she would escape and get onto land one way or another. By now she had heard a lot more about Virginia from the other prisoners. It was mainly populated by monsters called Salvages who had their faces in their bellies and no heads. Besides that, there were bears, lions, tigers, and possibly dragons, although no one was sure about these last creatures.

Then, one day, the land became invisible: first to Molly, whose eyesight had never been very good at a distance, and then to the other women, and finally to the sailors, who could see land when no one else could. Molly felt a stinging sense of loss. She stopped hoping that the ship might turn around—she knew now that it wouldn't.

A man called the Houndsditch Hellhound kept count of the days by scratching marks on one of the ship's beams with the edge of his manacles. He made extra-long marks for Sundays, and always announced loudly to the other prisoners what day of the week it was, and what date, and how many weeks they had been at sea. People shouted "Stow your widdes!" and "The devil take ye!" but he kept doing it. Sometimes it seemed to Molly that he was announcing the same dates over and over again—how else could March possibly last so long? Other times it seemed as if he were announcing two or three Sundays in a row, with no weekdays in between them. Molly wasn't sure whether this meant the Houndsditch Hellhound was crazy or that she was.

Either way, days and weeks had gone by. England was getting farther and farther away, and Virginia was getting closer. Molly would have to find a way to get home from there. London had begun to seem vague. Molly knew that there had once been paving stones beneath her feet instead of the rotting layer of curving wood that held back the endless ocean, that she had once been able to wander for miles through London's narrow, winding streets instead of being closed into a wooden world twenty wobbly paces wide. Especially, she knew that there had been other things to eat— sometimes—besides the rock-hard ship's biscuits and the half-rotten pickled beef. But it was all very far away now. And she'd have to get even farther away from it, to the strange and wild place called America, before she could find her way back.

In London, Molly knew the rules, how to get along. In America, she wouldn't know anything.

"It's the tigers and all that I'm most worried about," Mrs. Wilkes told her one gray, drizzly day as they huddled in the hold. "I don't mind the Salvages. It's none of my business where they keep their eyeballs at, as long as you can talk to 'em and reason with 'em like Christians."

She glanced at Molly.

"I mean, like folks," she amended.

"Are you going to try to get home?" said Molly.

"Bless you, no! Don't you know what happens to you if you go back to London?"

Molly shook her head.

"You show your petticoats to the crowd, that's what," said a woman called Whitefriars Sally. And in case Molly missed her meaning, she made a gesture as though jerking a noose around her neck. "Mind you, people do go back all the same. And then it's up to the judge to prove they're the same people as was sent, you know, and ofttimes he can't."

Mrs. Wilkes looked at the woman severely. "And ofttimes he can." She turned to Molly. "Don't you be trying it, love."

Molly said nothing. She would try to get home, of course. It was her only chance to survive.

Molly sat in the dark, stinking hold of the *Good Intention* and remembered the night she'd been caught. There was no police force in London, just a few elderly constables and watchmen. So the flat whose pocket you'd picked had to find you himself, and then find a constable willing to come with him to make the arrest. That was one of the things that made it easier for folks on the canting lay—folks like Molly and Hesper and Mrs. Wilkes—to make a living in London.

Molly had sensed her pursuers before she'd seen them—two nib culls in silken coats coming purposefully toward her in Fleet Market, with an old constable shuffling along behind them. She didn't recognize their faces, but then she never looked at a flat's face when she was picking his pocket. There was no reason to.

That same day, she'd filed the cly and gotten clean away with a silver scout, a watch she'd sold for two grunters to a fencing cull in Cock Lane. She remembered the crush of the crowd, smelling of sweat and dogs. She didn't remember seeing any faces, only pockets—a whole crowd of pockets, right at her eye level. Worsted broadcloth pockets, embroidered silk pockets, ragged pouches of sackcloth. She knew her way around all those kinds of pockets, which ones were lined and which ones weren't, the feel of each kind of cloth on her fingers— and which ones might have fishhooks sewn inside to catch pickpockets. She'd never actually seen a fishhooked pocket, let alone put her hand in one, but she'd heard stories.

At first she'd chosen a pocket that had a bulge in it, the right size for a purse. It had had no lining, which made things more difficult. There was no way to put your hand in a flat's pocket and not have him feel it, unless the flat was thinking of something else. So she had waited patiently for the dogfight to get really exciting, for all the people that had money bet on the outcome to crush closer and closer together, their attention completely on the dogs and not on their pockets.

Then a great green-and-gold carriage with some nobleman's crest painted on the side tried to push its way through the mob watching the dogfight. The crowd had jostled and shoved each other to get out of the way, and Molly lost sight of the pocket she'd planned to pick. In the crush, someone knocked over one of the men carrying a sedan chair. The chair had overturned in front of the horses, spilling its occupant, and the horses had spooked and reared up on their hind legs, sending everyone scrambling in different directions to escape the flailing hooves.

That was when the flat with the watch had backed up against Molly. Keeping her hands low and out of sight, Molly had carefully lifted the flap of his pocket and worked the thin satin pocket lining gently upward between her thumb and forefinger. If there was a lining, you never put your hand into the pocket at all; you just had to turn the lining inside out. The watch emerged on its own, and Molly deftly plucked out the pin that fixed the chain to the lining.

If she'd had an Adam-tiler—an accomplice—as many pickpockets did, she would have handed the watch to him in the same motion. But Molly worked alone, because she trusted no one. Instead, she slid the watch under her apron and let the movement of the crowd carry her away. The whole thing had taken less time than it takes to drink a sip of ale and wipe your mouth, and she'd gotten away with it as she had hundreds of times before. So why were they coming after her this time?

Someone had turned her in, that's why, Molly thought angrily. She swerved, letting the nibs and the constable see her turn into an alley, the beginning of the maze of alleys above Cow Lane. She ducked through a hidey-hole that wasn't visible from where they were. Someone had blown the gab, that's what; someone who knew her.

She slid between two leaning, dripping cold stone walls, along a crevice barely a foot wide. The nibs couldn't follow her even if they knew where she was. They were too well fed. But who'd squeaked on her? Was it the fencing cull she'd sold the watch to? Some of them were crooked all right, advertising that they could "find" stolen items for a reward. Molly had been going to Scotch Ben for a year, ever since her last fencing cull had danced the Tyburn hornpipe, but that didn't mean Scotch Ben hadn't decided to shop her now for the forty-pound reward he'd get if she swung.

Molly turned the last twist of the narrow tunnel, came out into a damp cellar that smelled of mold and sewers, and felt a clawlike hand close on the back of her neck.

She turned, kicked, and butted her assailants with her head. The wooden sole of her clog connected with soft flesh and someone cried out in pain, but more hands grabbed her. A man slid back the hatch of a dark lantern, and out of the corner of her eye Molly saw a quick swish of ragged skirts as someone slid off into the shadows. The two nib culls had Molly by the arms. The more she struggled, the tighter they gripped.

The white-haired constable—he must have been seventy years old—was holding the lantern and staring at Molly with a mixture of boredom and dismay. "Are you sure this is the girl?" he asked.

One of the nibs said something in bleedin' nib lingo that Molly couldn't understand. Something like, What did it matter if he was sure?

"Very well, if you're willing to arrest her"—the constable paused to yawn hugely—"and don't mind seeing her hanged."

The nib cull either said that he did or didn't want Molly hanged—it was hard to understand his words—and that he wanted his watch back.

"Very well. You!" The constable reached out and grabbed Molly by the front of her collar, jerking her in a different direction from the way the nibs were pulling her. "Hold still. This gentleman is arresting you for taking his watch. We're going to the magistrate."

Molly bit the constable on the arm.

Sitting in the hold of the *Good Intention,* Molly gave up trying to figure out what she'd been nabbed for. The whole trial had been so hard to understand, with everyone talking nib lingo over her and around her and about her, and nobody ever explaining what anything meant. She remembered nothing anyone had said, nothing but fear and confusion and a sharp feeling of betrayal. For all she knew, they'd snabbled her for something she didn't even do, unlikely though that seemed.

One thing she was sure of, though. She'd never been caught picking a pocket, not caught red-handed. Someone had whiddled; someone had squeaked; someone had turned her in.

She thought about the last place she'd been living, in a cellar in an alley off Dirty Lane, near Seven Dials. The cellar was partitioned into rooms, and the room she was in belonged to Nan Kettle, who kept three bomen—or maybe one of them was her husband; Molly didn't ask—and a couple of kinchin-morts that she was teaching her trade to. Molly was supposed to pay Nan Kettle a cut of her earnings every week, but Molly didn't go out of her way to let Nan know how much she'd made, and Nan and her bomen were usually too drunk to tell one week from another. That was the best thing about the room. The worst was that Nan Kettle and her main boman (or maybe husband), Leaping Jack, would get jug-bit on gin at least every other night, and start screaming and throwing things at each other. Molly and the kinchin morts would have to run out of the cellar and find somewhere else to spend the night. Usually Molly crept in the pitch dark to a building on Drury Lane and crawled under the stone steps at the front. There was a small space just big enough for Molly, although it smelled of emptied chamber pots. Once she had woken up to feel the sharp little feet of a rat scurrying across her face.

Nan Kettle would almost certainly have squeaked on her, probably for the price of a penny dram of gin. So would the kinchin morts, and two of the bomen. Leaping Jack might not have—Molly had never actually heard him speak except in grunts.

Before Nan Kettle, Molly had lived for a few months with a gang in Dogwell Alley, in Whitefriars. There had been an upright-man who ran the place; as far as Molly knew, his only name was Mirk. Mirk had run a tight ship, requiring all the thieves to report to him every evening and give him what they'd taken that day. The next morning, he would give them each a few pence, which he claimed was their share of what the fencing cull had given him. Molly hadn't cared for that system, especially since Mirk had wanted her to work with an Adam-tiler, or at least a bulker to bump into flats for her while she filed their pockets. When Mirk was arrested, Molly had moved on before anyone else could tell her she had to stay. Would someone from Mirk's gang have cackled on her? Probably.

A lot of people would have, Molly thought. But then there were people who wouldn't ever turn anyone in, like Molly. Molly had never blown the gab on anyone. It simply wasn't her way. Mrs. Wilkes, Molly thought, was also a person who wouldn't. You got a feeling from people, somehow. You knew who would squeak and who wouldn't. There wasn't anything you could do about it, but you knew.

Every night of the voyage, Molly took her stockings off and slept with them pillowed against her face, breathing in the smell of damp wool instead of the smell of the ship. The stockings had been her mother's. For two years she had carried them tied up in her petticoat, until her legs had grown big enough for them. They were still a bit too large, but she cinched them tight to her garters and they stayed up. Once the stockings had smelled of Mama, a smell of coal smoke and boiled furmity porridge, of gin and the cheap perfume that Mama's men friends had sometimes brought her. It was the smell

Molly had grown up with, and it felt like home. The smell had brought back the room she and Mama had shared in Seven Dials, and Molly had been able to close her eyes and imagine that Mama was just a few feet away and that when she opened her eyes, she'd see Mama's striped dress hanging on a nail on the wall. But that smell had vanished a long time ago. When Molly tried to remember it now, it was lost in the smell of sickness and fear, the smell that had sent her running into the street that night more than two years before.

Now the stockings were all she had of her mother's, so she held on to them tightly. One night in the hold, Molly was jerked awake by the tiny scratch of the woolen stockings moving against her cheek. The movement stopped. Molly held perfectly still and kept her breathing regular. After a moment, the stockings moved again. Molly clutched them tightly and yanked them toward her, at the same time kicking out hard with her left foot. She felt her foot hit somebody's kneecap, but the person made no noise, just crept quietly away. Hesper Crudge didn't have a real pickpocket's touch. You had to strike like lightning and be gone before the thunder. No wonder Hesper had been caught.

One day, there was excitement among the sailors up on deck. They were all gathered at the rail, pointing and talking. In the roped-off area at the stern where the prisoners were allowed to walk, Molly and the others gathered to peer over the rail.

"See?" One of the sailors pointed. "Land on the horizon. That's America."

Molly couldn't see anything, and said so.

The sailor drew near her, crouched down, and put his head close to Molly's. He pointed at the horizon, holding his arm at the level of her eyes. "See? Look where the ocean meets the sky."

Molly still couldn't see anything but the same cold steel-gray ocean she'd seen for two months. But she'd learned long ago never to reveal a weakness, so she said, "Oh, I see!"

The next day, seagulls were circling the ship, perching in the rigging and squawking loudly. That day Molly could see land. It was just a lumpy spot on the straight line of the horizon. It didn't look very promising, that American lump. Molly stared at the beginning of the seven-year sentence that she wished were already over.

"We're trying to make our first landfall at New York, on Manhattan island," said the same sailor who had spoken to Molly the day before.

Molly had never heard of New York. She didn't know that America had different places in it. She also didn't care, but since the sailor was still standing there, she said, "Is New York nice?"

"Oh, yes. It's the third-biggest city in America, you know, after Boston and Philadelphia. It has stone streets. Cookshops. Soft tommy. Everything."

"Soft tommy?"

"That's what sailors call fresh bread," the sailor explained. "Ship's biscuit is hardtack, and fresh bread is soft tommy."

Molly's stomach growled at the mention of fresh bread, and the sailor laughed.

Molly turned away angrily. She hated being laughed at.

"New York's all right," he said kindly. "Maybe you'll get sold there. You'll like it better than you would Maryland or the New England colonies."

Molly said nothing to that. She had no intention of staying, in New York or anywhere else in this America. As soon as she could, she would find a way to get back to England.

To Molly's disgust, the prisoners were ordered down into the hold. All day the ship tacked one way and then another. Overhead they heard the sailors running about, trimming sails and hauling ropes and cursing, the ship's rudder cranking as the men scrambled to avoid the shoals and hidden sandbars of the Narrows.

Molly felt eager to be on land again, eager to be anywhere but on this plaguey, stinking ship with its mad captain and miserable human cargo. But what good was it to be in New York? She wanted to be in London. London was what mattered. Molly thought with longing of the noise and smells and crowds of the London streets. To be part of those crowds again . . . London was where she belonged—prowling streets she had always known; finding her way through the ancient slums around Thieving Lane; slipping carefully through the mob at a hanging at Tyburn, or around the edges of a riot on Holbourne Hill; melting away into the thousands of passages and hidey-holes and secret stairways that the alleys concealed. There was always somewhere to run to, if the place you were in became too dangerous, or if the people there didn't treat you well. There was always something to steal, if you knew how, and a way to sell what you stole and get something to eat for it—well, usually, anyway. And you were free. Nobody told you what to do or when to do it; nobody cared where you were, or even noticed you were there, most of the time. As far as Molly was concerned, that was the only kind of life worth living.

Captain Mattock came below and ordered the women and girls to gather around him. "We're putting into New York for fresh water and provisions. Any of you I can sell in New York, I will. The rest will go on to Philadelphia, and to Virginia with the men if necessary."

"I thought we were all supposed to be taken to Virginia," someone said.

"Them fool judges in England think the whole of America is called Virginia," said Captain Mattock. "And nobody cares where I take you. Any more cork-brained questions? Good, then get yourselves fixed up. Try and look like something someone would want to buy if you don't want to spend another month at sea. And do something about the way you smell—you all stink."

With this helpful remark, he went back above.

Molly had never had an actual bath. She knew, as almost everyone did, that bathing was a foolish habit you could die of. But she did wash her face sometimes. She tried to do that now by spitting on the hem of her petticoat and rubbing her face with it. She and Mrs. Wilkes did their best to work the snarls out of each other's hair, and then Mrs. Wilkes plaited the wisps of Molly's black hair into two tight braids. She tore a strip off the bottom of her own petticoat and tied the braids at the end.

They arranged their clothes as neatly as they could, tucking and pulling, trying to hide stains and dirt. Molly pulled her precious too-big wool stockings smooth and cinched them to her garters. There were little sores on her hands and arms from scurvy, but nothing could be done about that.

"Put your clogs on, love," Mrs. Wilkes said.

"I've grown out of them," said Molly. They hadn't fit for several weeks. She could only get the front half of her foot into them. As soon as she started to take a step, the clogs came off.

"If we could just cut the leather a bit," Mrs. Wilkes said. But there was no way to cut it. Nobody had a knife.

The ship had stopped moving. The prisoners heard a heavy chain rattle across the deck above as the sailors dropped anchor. Night fell. Weren't they ever going to get off this plaguey ship? Molly took off her stockings, hid them in her bodice, and curled up to sleep.

In the morning, a sailor brought them the broken remains of hardtack biscuits. They were stale and moldy. Molly scraped idly at the green mold and picked a dead worm out of her biscuit with her fingernail. She thought longingly of a hot eel pie that she had once stolen from a cart in Honey Lane Market. It had been stuffed with currants and fat chunks of eel. She remembered the spicy-smelling steam that escaped when she bit into the crust, and the salty-sour lemon sauce running over her tongue.

"I suppose these biscuits will seem like a feast to us one day soon," said a woman morosely. She was called Jane Cutthroat; Molly didn't know if that was her real name.

"I hear there's lots to eat in this here America," the Houndsditch Hellhound said, clanking his chains.

"Aye, maybe there is, but not for us. The gentlefolk that buys us won't give us nothing but scraps we have to fight the dogs for."

"They can't all be like that, I'm sure," said Mrs. Wilkes. "And they buy us for seven years, you know, ducks. They'd lose money by starving us."

"That's just it. They have it all figured to the last farthing and crumb, them gentlefolks. Exactly how little they can feed us and still keep us alive. Most of us'll

drop dead on the last day of our service," said Jane
Cutthroat with gloomy satisfaction. "Seven years from
now, to the minute."

This last detail sounded unlikely to Molly, but the
rest sounded all too probable. People generally, she had
found, wanted what they could get out of you and would
give nothing they didn't have to. Molly was the same
way herself.

Four

With a scraping sound, the hatch was lifted off the hold. A square beam of morning sunlight streamed down on the prisoners.

"Get aloft—the women and girls only!" Captain Mattock called—unnecessarily, since the men and boys were still chained to the bulkheads. "One at a time."

Molly clambered stiffly to her feet. She took her stockings out of her bodice and fumbled for her clogs. They weren't there. She groped around on the deck.

"Have you seen my stamper cases?" she asked Mrs. Wilkes. But Mrs. Wilkes was searching for something in a bag she kept hidden under her petticoats, and only said "That's right, love."

Someone had taken them, Molly thought. Molly staggered to her feet again and made her way toward Hesper. All around her, women and girls were straightening and arranging their clothes, braiding each other's hair, and wrestling over possession of combs and scraps of handkerchief. Molly pushed through a mass of sour-smelling, clammy bodies, some of which pushed back.

Hesper was the kind of mort who'd stab a chiff in your back as soon as look at you—the kind of mort Molly survived by avoiding. But clogs were worth money, just like any other scowring-cheats. Molly glared down at Hesper, who seemed not to notice the commotion around her.

"Give me my shoes," Molly said.

Hesper didn't get up. "Shoes?" She sneered. "You have shoes? All I saw you in was some dirty old clogs."

"If they're so dirty, why'd you take them?"

"I don't have them." Hesper displayed her bare feet and spread her arms to show that she wasn't hiding anything.

Molly looked around in anger and frustration. "Who's got my bleedin' stamper cases?"

Nobody paid any attention. The women and girls were swarming toward the ladder, jostling and cursing. The men clanked their chains, as if trying to break free so they could follow. There was nothing Molly could do. Maybe Hesper hadn't taken the clogs. Molly was hungry and thirsty, and the air in the hold was stifling. The stench of unwashed bodies and sour clothes was worse than it had ever been. Molly turned her back on Hesper and joined the throng staggering up the ladder.

Up on deck, the sun was so bright Molly had to squeeze her eyes shut. Sailors were pushing her, herding the women and girls into a row.

Molly stuffed the stockings into her apron pocket. She opened her eyes little by little and looked around. In glimpses between the people crowding in front of her, over the ship's rail, she could see what looked like a little port town of brick, stone, and wood houses and shops, some with odd stair-stepped roofs. This was the third-biggest city in America? She could see from one side to the other. The streets had trees growing down the middle of them. Molly could see all the way up the wide street, from the dock to the open fields beyond. In the distance, a windmill turned slowly, its sails rising and falling above the tiled rooftops. Except for a star-shaped fort, there were no great buildings. From a tower inside the fort, the Union Jack flew. The sight of it startled Molly. To have traveled this far and still be under the British flag—how odd!

Would-be buyers began to board the ship, and somebody poked Molly sharply in the chest. "How much for this one? She's skinny; is there anything off for that?"

Then, suddenly, a woman grabbed Molly's lip and yanked at it, peering at her teeth. Molly drew back angrily and tried to bite her.

"Do you speak English?" a man asked Molly, looking

at her skeptically, as if she were a horse that would probably go lame or a barrel of flour that might turn out to be weevily.

"Do any of them speak Dutch?"

"Are these convicts? What did they do?"

"No," said Captain Mattock. "No prisoners here. These are all servants who come of their own free will."

What a lie, thought Molly.

"Are you a convict?" someone asked her. "What did you do?"

She couldn't see who had spoken to her, so she made a grim face, trying to look as much like a criminal as she could.

"I think this little black-haired one is simpleminded. Anything off the price for her being an idiot?"

"How long are they sold for?"

"Seven years," said Captain Mattock. "And the little ones until they reach their majority."

Majority? What did that mean?

"I want this one. How much for this one?" a man called. He had Hesper Crudge by the arm.

"I don't want to go with him. I'm allowed to say no," said Hesper.

Captain Mattock wheeled around. "Who told you that?"

Hesper smirked. "It's true, isn't it?"

The other women looked interested. So did the buyers. They all looked at Captain Mattock.

"You can say no twice," Captain Mattock admitted reluctantly. "If you say no twice, you must take the third person who offers for you willy-nilly."

"Well, I say no to this one. He stinks."

"Insolent baggage!" said the man, dropping Hesper's arm. Hesper flounced back into the row with a clump of her clogs.

Clogs? Molly looked at Hesper's feet. Hesper was wearing Molly's clogs.

"Hey!" Molly sprang forward and grabbed Hesper, too angry to worry about how dangerous Hesper could be. "Give me back my clogs!"

"Your clogs? These are *my* clogs." Hesper smiled sweetly.

Molly grabbed Hesper's shoulders and shook her. "Give them back, you bloody thief!"

Hesper wrenched herself away from Molly and slapped her. "Wench! I don't know what you're talking about."

Molly shoved Hesper, and they both went down.

"Excuse me!" said a loud, authoritative voice from the gangplank. Everybody looked.

"Bell!" Captain Mattock reached out and shook the hand of a tall man dressed in a powdered wig, a dark green coat, and knee breeches. "Good to see you again. I'll send my man around in the evening with our supply order."

"Fine, fine." Mr. Bell released the captain's hand and

stepped over Molly's and Hesper's prone figures. "I'm actually here on other business. I have word from my connections in London that you have a Jewish woman among the convicts you're selling." He took a letter from his coat pocket and proffered it to Captain Mattock.

"Convicts?" A woman who had been trying to examine Mrs. Wilkes's teeth turned and stared. "I thought you said they weren't convicts."

Captain Mattock glared at Mr. Bell. He took the letter and handed it to his mate. "I don't read so well in this light," he explained. "Beats me how you people always know these things. Anyway, she's for sale the same as the others, whoever she is."

"Abraham," said Mr. Bell. "According to my letter, the woman is a Mary Abraham."

Captain Mattock gestured impatiently at his mate. The mate was flipping through a stack of ink-smeared papers.

"I think that's me," said Molly in a small voice.

Mr. Bell was standing almost right over her. "You're the Jewish woman?"

"Well, I'm Molly Abraham." The man looking down at her was a nib cull, but not rich. Still, he was very clean—at least his white woolen stockings and his resoled brass-buckled shoes, at Molly's eye level, seemed to be. He was the sort of man whose pocket Molly wouldn't have bothered to pick because there wouldn't have been much in it and he probably would have caught her. But a gang of boys—a pack of wild, predatory street boys—would have hunted him. Or the rough coves around Whitefriars—they would have stolen his clothes, his wig, and his shoes, and thrown the rest of him into the river.

The man was looking at her thoughtfully. She suddenly felt small and very dirty, and she wished she'd had time to put on her stockings. She tucked her bare feet under her skirt and tried to flatten her hair down with one hand. It was all pulled out of the neat braids Mrs. Wilkes had made.

The mate pulled out a sheet of large, floppy paper. "Here it is, sir. Mary Abraham, a little girl, to be bound and indentured beyond the seas until she reaches her majority at age twenty-one."

"Twenty-one?" Molly cried.

"Of course," said the captain.

"That's the one," said Mr. Bell, nodding at Molly. He reached down and offered her his hand.

Molly stared at the hand, wondering what she was supposed to do with it. Then the hand took hold of her own, and Molly realized that the man was helping her to her feet. His hand felt warm and clean compared to the clammy skin of the prisoners. She stood up, smoothing her skirts and feeling, if possible, even smaller.

"Fifteen pounds sterling," said Captain Mattock. "I'll take good British pounds or regular New York currency.

Not those shell beads you New Yorkers are always using instead."

Fifteen pounds was a huge amount of money, more than Molly and her mother had ever had even after their best filches. She was surprised Captain Mattock thought she was worth it.

So was Mr. Bell. "She's awfully small," he commented.

Captain Mattock shrugged. "Feed 'em and they grow."

Mr. Bell looked at Molly. "Have you had the smallpox?"

Molly shuddered at the word, and quickly squelched the memories it brought with it. "Yes."

Mr. Bell nodded. "And not fair-spoken," he added to Captain Mattock.

Captain Mattock glared at Molly. "Say 'Yes, sir,' baggage," said Captain Mattock.

Molly said nothing and glared back.

"I think ten pounds would be quite enough," said Mr. Bell.

"Take it or leave it," said Captain Mattock. "I don't care who buys which of 'em. It's you Jews that always insist I sell the Jewish ones to you."

Mr. Bell thought for a moment. "I'll pay five pounds sterling, twelve bushels of Indian corn, and eight gallons of New England rum."

Captain Mattock scowled again. "I don't like your

Indian corn. I'm an Englishman, not a bloody New York."

"We New Yorkers are Englishmen too," Mr. Bell reminded him.

"Englishmen? Don't make me laugh. The other colonies may be English, but this town is like a hodge-podge quilt. Walloons, Huguenots, Africans, Spaniards—everything but Englishmen. Good New York wheat is the only corn I'll take."

"Very well, six bushels of peas and six of New York wheat."

"I can do better than that in Philadelphia. Make it twelve of New York wheat, and the devil take the peas."

"Eight of wheat, and a peck of lemons from Barbados."

Molly stared back and forth between the two of them. She had heard people bargaining like this in Bartholomew's Fair—for old clothes, for secondhand shoes, for pigs.

"Very well, eight. And the lemons, and the rum. And the money," said Captain Mattock.

Mr. Bell nodded his agreement. They shook hands.

"Give him her indenture," said Captain Mattock to the mate.

"This is New York colony," said the mate. "You have to go before a magistrate with the indentures; you can't just hand them over as you do in Virginia."

"I knew that!" Captain Mattock shook his fist at the

mate. "Do you think to teach me my business, you fool?" He turned back to Mr. Bell. "Anyway, you can take her now. We'll settle up later."

Mr. Bell nodded to Molly. "Get your things, then, Mary."

Molly felt a sudden panic. She had just been bought by the stranger in the powdered wig. She had been swept into the slavery that the other prisoners had talked about on the ship, the seven years of starvation and servitude that were either better or worse than the gallows, depending on whom you asked. She had no control over what was happening to her. She felt a sharp stab of longing for London, where there was always somewhere to run, always a new hiding place. Now things were being decided for her and there was nothing she could do.

But she did have a choice, she realized. She could refuse to go with Mr. Bell. Hesper had said they could refuse, and Captain Mattock had grudgingly agreed.

She looked around at the strangers who were still poking and prodding their prospective servants. Mr. Bell hadn't poked her once, nor peered at her teeth. She looked up at him again.

"Get your things, Mary," he repeated.

"I don't have any things," she said.

Mr. Bell looked at her feet. "Where are your shoes?"

Molly nodded at Hesper Crudge. "She's got 'em."

Mr. Bell turned back and said something to Captain

Mattock, who was arguing with another customer about the price of Mrs. Wilkes.

"The shoes go with the girl," said Captain Mattock. "If you want the shoes, you have to buy the other girl."

Mr. Bell glanced at Hesper. "I don't want another girl. I can barely afford this one." To Hesper he said, "Come, now, off with those shoes. Don't you know what it says in the Bible about stealing?"

"No," said Hesper, smirking. "Bleedin' autem-cove, ain't you, talking about Bibles." She laughed, a single short "Ha!"

Molly didn't know what the Bible said about stealing either, but she knew that whatever it was, it wasn't likely to get her shoes back for her.

Mr. Bell shrugged. "Well, there's nothing to be done about it, Mary. Come along. I'll take you home to my wife."

Molly couldn't believe it. Wasn't he going to make Hesper give the shoes back? It would be easy for him; he was bigger than Hesper.

But Mr. Bell had started down the gangplank. Molly looked at him doubtfully. Who was he, and what would happen to her if she went with him? He seemed much more human than the imaginary gentlefolk Jane Cutthroat had been talking about the day before. It was *possible* he was going to beat her and starve her, but she wasn't planning to stay with him long, anyway. And she was eager to be on land. She might as well go.

She started down the gangplank, then remembered she hadn't said goodbye to Mrs. Wilkes. She looked back and waved, but Mrs. Wilkes was arguing with Captain Mattock and didn't see her.

As soon as Molly stepped off the gangplank, dizziness overcame her. The stone cobbles of the pier seemed to be rocking up and down. She tried to take a step and everything seemed to lurch. She fell down on the stones.

"You've got your sea legs yet," said Mr. Bell, reaching down for her. "There, just stand still. We'll wait a bit and it'll pass." He reached into his coat, pulled out a watch, looked at it, and then looked up at the ship's mast. He squinted in the sun. He had lines around his eyes and around his mouth. "Have you any schooling, Mary?"

"No," said Molly. She didn't even know anybody who had been to school.

"Can you read?"

"No." Molly scowled. He must be trying to make her look stupid. The ground was still pitching and spinning, and her eyes wouldn't focus.

"Mary is an unusual name for a Jew," said Mr. Bell. "We'll call you Miriam, your Hebrew name."

"My name is Molly," Molly snapped. "And my mother gave it to me."

"I had this letter from our people in London that you would be on the *Good Intention*." He gestured at the folded paper again; Molly wished he would hold still. "They said you had been convicted of stealing a handkerchief."

That startled Molly. "Filching a handkerchief? I'm no bleedin' stook-hauler."

"Of course not. Well, the prosecutor probably said it was a handkerchief because stealing one needn't always be a hanging crime. That's why they often charge the smaller ones with that instead of what they really did." Mr. Bell looked at her and waited.

The ground was beginning to calm down. The horrible dizziness in Molly's head was receding. She wondered vaguely why Mr. Bell understood Flash-cant. No nib cull ought to.

"What did you steal?" Mr. Bell asked.

Molly didn't answer.

"Very well," said Mr. Bell. "Can you cook?"

"No," said Molly.

"You must say 'No, sir,' " said Mr. Bell.

Molly didn't answer.

Mr. Bell waited some more. He seemed to be good at that. Molly found it annoying. People in London didn't watch you and wait for you to talk; they watched you and wondered whether you were going to need killing. At least you knew what was on their minds.

"No, sir," she muttered, finally. What did it matter?

"Hmm. What can you do?"

Molly thought. She knew how to cut the pocket from a lady's girdle without the lady feeling a thing. She could tell from the stitching on the outside whether a pocket had a lining and, from the way the cloth draped, whether there was anything in the pocket and how heavy it was. She knew how to tell the difference between silver and base metal. She could tell a country clown from a London cove by the way they walked. She knew the importance of watching people's eyes, and their hands. She knew the whole maze of tunnels and secret doors and hatches around Seven Dials, and she knew how to lose herself in a crowd instead of running away.

"Nothing," she said.

"Come, at your age you must know something. Can you light a fire?"

"Of course," said Molly.

Mr. Bell waited.

"Of course, sir," said Molly grumpily.

"And can you wash clothes?"

"*Wash* 'em?" said Molly.

Mr. Bell smiled. The smile fit into the wrinkles around his eyes and mouth, and his face suddenly looked kind. Before she could stop herself, Molly was smiling back.

"Let's go," said Mr. Bell. "This is Broad Street, and my house is right up here on Mill Street, near the synagogue. My wife is at home."

The cobblestones of the Manhattan streets were cleaner than the London ones, but they were cold, and

Molly's bare feet ached. Pigs snuffled, looking for garbage to eat, and they passed a cow grazing on a green patch in the middle of the street. There were carriages here and there, but no sedan chairs for carrying wealthy ladies about so they could protect their gowns from the mud. Most of the people walked. There were trees beside the street, and a few tulips growing beneath them.

"It's spring," said Mr. Bell. "Passover was two weeks ago. You've probably lost track of time on that ship, haven't you?"

Molly had no idea what Passover was, but she realized it had been a very long time since her trial. "It was winter in London," she said.

"You'll find the winters colder here. But there's no need to worry about that for months yet." He looked down at her and smiled again. "I'm from London too, you know."

Molly stared at him. So he was from London and he understood Flash-cant. But he was too clean and well-spoken to be on the canting lay. She said the first thing that came into her head: "Why don't you go back?" Then, to keep him smiling, she added, "Sir."

He shrugged. "This is home now. And it's a better place for us, you know. England's not bad for us, but New York is even better."

Molly wondered what he meant by "us." His wife and himself, she supposed.

"It's more free," he went on. "Look around you. There are all sorts of people here. We're just one more sort, and nobody cares too much."

Molly looked around. There were certainly all kinds of people. Not as many people as in London, of course, but they all looked as if they had come from different places. Molly saw people who looked English, some dressed in ordinary English clothes and some in buckskins. She saw people she was sure must be Indians, though some of them were wearing English clothes. There were swaggering men in high-topped boots and plumed beaver hats who wore swords at their sides. And there were women in round Dutch skirts and wooden shoes. And Africans, lots of Africans. Far more Africans than she had ever seen in London. New York must be very close to Africa, Molly thought.

There were not, however, any Salvages without heads and with faces in their bellies. Molly suspected that there weren't any of those in New York. And now that she thought about it in broad daylight, with her feet on the ground, probably not anywhere else either.

Five

The Bells' house was small and made of bricks, with a stair-stepped gable end facing the street. The date 1654 was set in wrought iron near the roof. There was just enough space separating the house from the houses next door for a person to walk around it to the back. There was a front door up three stone steps, but Mr. Bell led Molly through one of the narrow alleys to the back. He pushed open a gate in the board fence, and Molly followed him into a dirt yard that was partly paved with bricks. The back door of the house burst open, and three women came out. One was rather stout, with a floppy white cap and sky-blue eyes. The second was African, with skin the color of the sea-soaked wood of the *Good Intention*'s hold, her hair cut close to her head. The African woman was carrying a little girl about three years old, who had eyes of the same sky blue as the first woman's and blond curls that poked out from under her cap. The third woman was thin and sharp-boned, with smooth, hard hair the color of steel visible under her cap. She had the closed, angry expression of someone who is always looking for the worst in everybody and usually manages to find it. Molly instinctively cringed at the sight of the steel-haired woman. She hoped that this was not Mrs. Bell.

"So it was true, Ephraim," said the blue-eyed woman. "But goodness, she's just a little girl. How could they?"

Mr. Bell shrugged. "It's the law, Hannah. The law of England, which for better or worse is our country. And now Miriam has come to us, for which we must thank God."

And to Molly's surprise, he put on his head the three-cornered hat he had been carrying and began praying in another language. Embarrassed, Molly looked away. She examined the yard she was standing in. She saw a woodpile, and a wooden privy, and a table that held a tin tub and a pile of dishes.

"Amen," said the blue-eyed woman, whom Molly had decided with relief must be Mrs. Bell. "Well, come in, Miriam. You must want a bath after all that time on the ship."

Mrs. Bell put an arm around Molly's shoulders and ushered her into the house. The other women followed, but Mr. Bell slipped away. Inside was a brick-floored kitchen with a table and benches, a brick fireplace, and a big wooden cabinet that seemed to be a bed. A fire crackled and glowed in the fireplace, giving off a sweet, smoky smell that reminded Molly of bonfires on Guy Fawkes Day. It took her a moment to realize that the smoke had a pleasant smell because what was burning was wood, not coal.

The African woman put the little girl down and dragged a large wooden tub from under the bed. The little girl toddled over to Molly and stood staring up at her, her fingers in her mouth. Molly stared back. She had never seen a child that age so clean.

The steel-haired woman looked at Molly and said something to Mrs. Bell in a language Molly did not know.

"Yes, she is from London," said Mrs. Bell. "You knew she was coming. We all talked about it, remember?"

The steel-haired woman said something else.

"Let's speak English, Adah," said Mrs. Bell. "Since it's a language we all understand."

Adah shrugged. "I just wonder that you would want to have one of them in your household, that's all. With little Rachel to take a bad influence. And David."

Mrs. Bell pursed her lips. "I've never seen any signs of David taking a bad influence," she said curtly.

"You never know at that age," said Adah.

Mrs. Bell sighed. "Miriam, this is Mrs. Grip. I am

Mrs. Bell, and this"—she indicated the African woman—"is Arabella. And the little one is Rachel. You know why we took Miriam, Adah. Miriam is Jewish."

"So was Moses Susman," said Adah. "And look what happened to him."

"You must take one of our pickles with you when you go, Mrs. Grip," said Arabella, going into a pantry closet beside the bed and coming back with a shiny, wet green pickled cucumber.

"We'll be seeing you in the synagogue on Saturday," said Mrs. Bell.

Adah ignored both of these hints. "I hate to see you nursing a viper at your bosom, that's all. You're too kind and trusting, and so is your Ephraim."

Mrs. Bell reddened slightly. "Ephraim knows what he's doing."

In London, Molly had once seen a man locked in a pillory who was enduring the usual hour of having horse dung and rotten vegetables thrown at him when a woman came forward and slapped him in the face with a dead mackerel. The man couldn't move his head or his hands to defend himself, of course, so he looked straight ahead, his expression unchanging, while the woman kept beating him in the face with the fish. Hunks of fetid flesh flew in all directions and clung to the man's face while he stared steadily at the woman, giving her a look that said she was something less worthwhile than a dead mackerel herself. He never spoke or changed his expression, even when she was down to the bare fish skeleton and a few foul bits of fin and was still thwacking him on the nose. And then she wilted under his gaze and stopped, the fish skeleton drooping in her hand, and turned and slunk away. She'd tried to put a little bounce into her walk, as if she'd been meaning to leave then all along, but it was a slink and there was no disguising it.

Molly tried to look at Adah Grip the way that man had looked at the mackerel woman.

Adah didn't seem to notice. "Well, maybe he does. It's one thing to perform a mitzvah and another to put your own children at risk. And I think it's a wicked shame that those judges keep dumping the scum of the London streets on His Majesty's law-abiding subjects in America. What did she do, anyway?"

Arabella came forward and thrust the dripping pickle into Adah's hand, and Mrs. Bell said, "Look what time it's getting to be. It's a shame you can't stay longer, Adah." The two of them edged her firmly out the kitchen door by standing a little too close to Adah so that she backed up, and then standing a little too close to her again. It was expert maneuvering. They must have had a lot of practice.

The door closed on Adah Grip while she was still offering her opinion about Molly.

"Never mind her, Miriam," said Mrs. Bell, lifting a kettle of hot water off the hob and emptying it into the washtub.

"Spiteful old thing," said Arabella, bringing a bucket of cold water and pouring it on top of the hot. A cloud of steam rose from the tub, making Molly cough.

"She's been very unhappy since her husband died of the smallpox," Mrs. Bell said.

"Yes, and before that too," said Arabella. "Come on, Miriam, off with your things."

Molly backed away, horrified. "Off with my what?"

"Your things," said Mrs. Bell, bringing a small wooden tub of jellied soap. "You can't take a bath in your clothes, dear."

"I don't take baths," said Molly firmly.

"Everybody takes baths," said Arabella. "You'll feel much better for it." She undid the ties on Molly's dress, and it fell off before Molly knew what had happened. Molly ducked her head and butted Arabella in the stomach. Arabella stumbled backward but didn't fall. She dealt Molly a clout on the ear.

Molly stood, holding her burning ear and seething. Arabella was too big for Molly to fight. New York was like London in that way at least. Adults could hit you and there was nothing you could do about it.

"Nobody's going to hurt you," said Mrs. Bell, as if Arabella hadn't just hit Molly. "Just take off your shift and get into the tub, and then we have some things of mine we have cut down for you to put on."

Not going to hurt her? They were trying to *kill* her! "People die of baths!" Molly said.

"Not in May, they don't," said Arabella. "Come on now, off with your shift and jump in."

"I ain't taking off my mish," said Molly. "I never have." She raised her fists, but she could see it was no use. There were two of them, not counting the baby, and they were bigger than her.

"Miriam, please," said Mrs. Bell.

There seemed to be no getting around it. They had her cornered. This was worse than anything they had predicted on the ship. Her face burning, Molly quickly pulled her shift up over her head. Ducking her head so she didn't have to look at any of them, she stepped into the bath and sat down quickly.

The water was flaming hot. It was like being boiled alive. She gasped but stayed sitting down, because the alternative was to stand up naked. The hot water made the scurvy sores on her arms sting. She saw little Rachel watching her with interest. She could have done without that.

A moment later, she felt something cold glop down on her head.

They were washing her hair! Molly felt her throat contract in terror. She had known people who had died of having baths, but she had never known anyone who had ever dared to wash their hair.

"Stop it! You're killing me!" she squawked, batting at Arabella with her hands.

Arabella did stop. "Did I get soap in your eyes?"

"No, you're washing my hair! You'll get my brain wet and I'll die!"

"Oh, you will not," said Arabella, continuing to lather up Molly's hair. "That's an old wives' tale. Look at me; I've washed my hair plenty of times and I'm not dead, am I?"

Molly was about to reply when she caught sight of Mrs. Bell gathering up her fallen clothes. She leapt to her feet, water cascading from her body and splashing on Arabella's dress and apron. "Get your plaguey fambles off my duds!"

Mrs. Bell looked at her in surprise. "I have to burn these, Miriam," she said calmly. "I'm afraid even the ragman won't want them."

"You leave my scowring-cheats alone!" Molly jumped out of the tub, knocking it over, and fell, sprawling on the brick floor in a sea of soapy water. Molly scraped her palms, but she ignored the pain, scrambled to her feet, and grabbed the bundle in Mrs. Bell's arms. Molly wrested it from her, threw it to the floor, and dug the gray woolen stockings out from the apron pocket.

"Really, Miriam!" said Mrs. Bell.

"Keep your grubby mitts off my stockings!" said Molly. She clutched the stockings tightly against her chest and backed into the corner beside the fireplace, her right hand balled in a fist. She was completely naked and sopping wet, and her hair was full of soapsuds and was sticking out all over the place. She felt more helpless than she had felt since the day she had waited for the judge to sentence her. But there was no way anyone was going to get her mother's stockings.

Mrs. Bell looked a little stunned but was trying not to show it. "Miriam, those stockings are very dirty. I'm not sure they'll come clean. And they have holes in them," she said calmly.

Arabella had the same expression of studied calm. She was kneeling beside the fallen washtub, her dress and apron drooping into the pool of soapy water. Rachel clung to Arabella with one hand while putting the other one almost completely into her mouth.

Mrs. Bell dropped her hands to her sides. "Don't you want to be clean, dear?"

"You're not getting my stockings, so clear off," said Molly.

"They're a mess, Miriam. And they smell of the ship. You can knit new ones. I'll teach you how."

"My name's not Miriam, it's Molly. And the stockings are mine."

"All right, Molly," said Mrs. Bell. She waited.

Molly waited too, but she unclenched her fist. There was no point in trying to fight Mrs. Bell. She was taller than Molly, with the strong arms of a hardworking woman, even though her gentle face and kind blue eyes told Molly she hadn't been in many fights. But even if

Molly could take her, there was still Arabella. Arabella was small but tough-looking. And besides, they both had clothes on, which did seem to give a person a certain advantage.

"Wouldn't you like to learn to knit, Molly?" said Mrs. Bell. "I have some lovely scarlet wool."

"No!" said Molly. If they took the stockings from her, she would have nothing left at all from London, from home, from the room in Seven Dials that she had shared with Mama.

Maybe she couldn't fight these women, but she could cling to the stockings with all the strength in her pocket-picking hands.

Mrs. Bell shrugged. "Well, all right. Then you'll have to learn to darn. You'll need to wash those stockings and then darn up all those holes."

And she turned away. Molly came carefully out of the corner, not sure if this was a trap, but Mrs. Bell didn't spin quickly to hit her or try to take the stockings.

The kitchen door opened and a boy came into the room for less than a second. Molly had an impression of curly brown hair and a very red face, and then he was gone again, slamming the door behind him.

"Oh dear, was that David?" said Mrs. Bell, turning to look at the door.

"I think so," said Arabella. "Come on, Molly, we're

going to have to rinse your hair out with cold water, since there isn't any more hot."

When Molly was finally soap-free and feeling rather chilly, Arabella gave her a piece of sackcloth to dry off with, and Mrs. Bell brought out a white petticoat and shift and a blue woolen dress.

"These were mine," Mrs. Bell explained. "I'm afraid we didn't cut them down enough. We were expecting a bigger girl. But we'll just baste it up for now."

When they were done, Molly found herself encased in more cloth than she could ever remember being in in her life, and she was, she realized, as clean as the Bells. She felt a sharp sense of loss, as if something important had been taken from her. They had washed her and dressed her in their clothes, and she realized now they could do whatever they liked to her. They had bought her. She pulled her mother's stockings onto her feet, knotted them at the top so that they would stay up, and then immediately stepped into a puddle and got the bottoms soaking wet.

"We're late getting dinner," said Mrs. Bell. "Molly, take the broom and sweep all that water out the door."

Mrs. Bell and Arabella started to get busy with something at the table, and Rachel crawled around on the brick floor, popping soap bubbles with her finger. Molly pulled off her wet stockings and hung them over the back of a bench, then went and got the straw broom that Mrs. Bell had pointed out and looked at the water. How were you supposed to sweep water?

Experimentally, she swept the broom across the deepest water. A wave rolled across the floor and splashed Rachel, who jumped back delightedly and then sat down in the puddle.

Fortunately, no one had noticed that Molly had gotten Rachel all wet. Molly tried to sweep again, this time sending the wave away from Rachel's direction. Rachel gave a whoop and chased after the wave on her hands and knees, then flopped down flat on her stomach in the soapy water.

Arabella turned around. "Rachel, get out of the puddle. Molly, you're holding that broom wrong."

Molly threw the broom down angrily. They had bought her and thrown her clothes away and washed her and made her look like a stranger to herself, and now they were taunting her with impossible tasks and even criticizing the way she held a broom! She had had enough.

She was just about to say so when the door opened and the boy came in again. His face turned a bit red when he saw Molly, but much less red than before, now that she had clothes on. He smiled at her. Molly backed up against the wall by the fireplace. She did not like boys. This boy was about fourteen years old, with curly, unpowdered brown hair and laughing black eyes. Molly could only assume he was laughing at the thought of how much fun he was going to have beating her up.

Rachel jumped up, dripping, and cried, "Davey!" She charged across the room toward the boy, and he scooped her up in his arms just before they collided.

"Oh, you're all wet, Rachey!" said the boy, laughing. Rachel responded by untying the black ribbon that held back his curly hair.

Molly did not find David's laughter reassuring. Boys were the most dangerous people there were. Men and women usually ignored you, and other girls seldom bothered to hurt you unless you had something they wanted—or unless they were like Hesper Crudge. But boys would hurt you for fun. It was a game to them.

The poor boys around Seven Dials were the worst, because they were almost impossible to escape. They knew the hidey-holes and alleys and secret passages as well as she did. The rich boys, the sons of the gentry and nobility, went around in a gang called the Mohocks. They beat up elderly city watchmen and slashed people's faces with knives, but they were usually too drunk to catch Molly. The boys who were neither rich nor poor, the apprentices, were better runners than the Mohocks. They didn't carry knives, but they threw rocks. As long as Molly could outrun them long enough to reach some alley or lane that they were afraid to enter, she would be safe. Ragged, half-starved pickpockets like Molly were accepted in places where a clean, well-fed apprentice would be lucky to escape with his life.

This boy looked like one of those apprentices, and she was in his territory. Molly pressed against the wall so hard that she could feel the bricks digging into her back.

"Hello," said the boy, still smiling.

Molly said nothing. She put her fists up, ready to try to fight, and looked over at the women at the table.

"Molly, that's David," said Mrs. Bell. "David, this is Molly. The girl your father told you about."

Molly put her fists down but continued to watch David warily.

"David won't hurt you, Molly," said Arabella.

David laughed, but then looked at Molly's face and stopped. "No, of course I won't. Rachel here is the one you have to watch out for. She's the dangerous one. Rachey, give me that ribbon back."

"No!" said Rachel, and she struggled so hard that David had to put her down. He tried to grab the ribbon out of her hand, but she ran across the room, shrieking with laughter. David chased after her. Molly did not find that encouraging.

When Mr. Bell returned home a few minutes later, he was in a very bad mood. Molly noticed this right away. She was surprised Mrs. Bell didn't. In London, noticing when people were in a bad mood was an important skill for staying alive.

"What is this mess?" he said, looking around the kitchen. Molly was still sweeping the water here and there without really getting it anywhere. Arabella had taken Rachel upstairs to change into something dry, and David had gone to get more water. Mrs. Bell was stirring soup over the fire.

"The bathwater spilled," said Mrs. Bell. "Dinner's going to be a little late."

"I don't have time for dinner to be late. I have work to get back to," said Mr. Bell. "And so does David. Where's David?"

"Hauling water," said Mrs. Bell.

"Why can't Arabella do that? Why can't Molly do that? Where's Arabella?"

Mrs. Bell dropped the wooden spoon into the soup kettle and turned around. "We've been having a difficult morning, Ephraim."

"So have I. Things have been crazy over at the warehouse. How difficult can it be to get dinner ready by twelve o'clock?"

"Try it sometime!" Mrs. Bell snapped, her hands on her hips. "Try it with a three-year-old running around and a new girl fresh off the boat who needs bathing and dressing. And you, just disappearing as soon as you'd dumped her on me!"

Arabella and Rachel came downstairs just as David came in, setting down two sloshing buckets of water. He eyed his mother and father warily.

"With two servants to help you, I don't see why you can't get it done without sending my son out to haul water like a woman!" Mr. Bell snapped back.

David rolled his eyes. Molly could tell he wanted to be left out of this. She did too. But she wasn't.

"I don't have two servants to help me; I have Arabella and a little girl who's exhausted from two months at sea," said Mrs. Bell. "You think I should send her out to haul water? She doesn't even have any shoes!"

Molly looked at the table. Arabella had been slicing cheese, and the sharp iron knife was still lying there. In Molly's experience, conversations like this usually ended in blows, and if there was a knife around, it often ended up buried in someone's flesh. She edged toward the table.

"Besides, who ever decided that it's women's work to get water?" said Mrs. Bell. "Water is heavy. You try carrying it for once and you'll see what I mean."

In Seven Dials, that was the sort of remark that usually caused a cove to start beating his mort. After that, the boy would probably join in, taking one side or the other, and anything heavy, sharp, or movable would be put to use as a weapon. Molly grabbed the knife and, clutching it tightly in front of her, backed up against the table.

Silence fell in the room. Everyone stared at Molly.

"Molly, child!" said Mrs. Bell finally. She looked

stunned, making no effort to hide it. So did Mr. Bell and David. They all seemed to have frozen, like statues.

"Molly, give me that knife at once," said Mr. Bell.

Molly shook her head. She didn't want anyone to get stabbed; she had seen it happen too many times. She looked away from Mr. Bell, and back at David. She and David looked at each other. David took a deep breath and seemed to go very calm.

"It's all right," said David. "Molly doesn't want to hurt anyone." He looked at Molly. "You don't want to hurt anyone, do you?"

Molly looked at him. Of course she didn't. She was trying to stop someone from getting hurt. She held the knife tightly by the handle, in front of her chest.

"Sometimes people quarrel," said David. "It probably seems scary if you're not used to it."

Molly still didn't answer. Did he think she wasn't used to it? After the quarreling came fighting, usually. Then stabbing.

"Will you give me the knife, Molly?"

Molly shook her head. She actually felt foolish holding the knife now that everyone had gone quiet and Mr. and Mrs. Bell had stopped arguing. But she would feel even more foolish giving the knife to David. It wasn't as if she had actually been about to do anything with it.

"Or how about if you put the knife back on the table."

That seemed like a reasonable suggestion. Molly turned around and set the knife down, exactly where she'd found it.

The three Bells relaxed visibly. Molly hadn't realized they would all be so upset when she grabbed the chiff. In London, it would have been a perfectly normal and sensible thing to do.

"Molly, don't you ever . . . ," Mrs. Bell began.

Mr. Bell interrupted. "It was my fault, not Molly's. I was the one who disturbed the peace of the home. I'm sorry."

"And I'm sorry I snapped at you," said Mrs. Bell.

There was silence. They seemed to be waiting for Molly to say something.

"I wasn't going to use the bleedin' chiff," she said. "It was just what the cove there—what David said. And I thought someone might, you know."

They didn't seem to understand. Molly had the strange feeling that they might actually have never seen a fight with knives. But that seemed impossible.

"No harm done," said Mrs. Bell.

Mrs. Bell had set a tin washbasin, a dipper, and a handkerchief on the table, and Mr. Bell poured water over his hands, then lifted them up and said a prayer. The others did the same. Mrs. Bell beckoned to Molly.

"I just had a bath," Molly said.

"Shush!" said Arabella, and pushed Molly to the basin. Molly scowled and decided this was one more thing she would have to put up with. She poured water over her hands. Arabella held up three fingers, and Molly figured that meant that she was supposed to pour the water over her hands three times. Nobody was talking.

They all circled the table, and Mr. Bell picked up a loaf of bread and said a prayer over it. Molly could smell the soup in the steaming pot set in the middle of the table. She wanted to scoop up a dipperful of soup from the pot and drink it, but everybody was just standing there in silence. Finally, Mr. Bell finished the prayer and broke pieces of bread from the loaf, giving them to everybody. Molly ate hers so fast that her throat ached.

Mrs. Bell was ladling soup into wooden bowls. As soon as Molly's bowl was handed to her, she raised it to her mouth and started slurping out of it. David stared at her, then looked away hastily.

"Use a spoon, Molly," Mrs. Bell said quietly, pointing to a round pewter spoon at Molly's place on the table. Molly put her bowl down, embarrassed. The others were eating their soup with spoons—even Rachel, who was also managing to dribble quite a bit on her clean smock. Molly dipped the spoon into the bowl. It was slow work, lifting the soup to her mouth in tiny little spoonfuls, but finally Molly managed to empty her bowl. To her surprise, Mrs. Bell immediately took it from her and filled it again. The Bells didn't even push each other away to grab the food; there was as much of it as anybody wanted. There was more bread, and pickles, and jam. After a while, Molly actually stopped eating because she wasn't hungry anymore. The feeling was an odd one. Her stomach felt stretched out and heavy.

When dinner was over, Mr. Bell and David went back to work, and Arabella started piling up dishes to carry outside to wash.

"Just take this water out for Arabella, Molly," said Mrs. Bell, lifting a black cast-iron kettle down from the pothook over the fireplace.

Molly went to the raised stone hearth and took the kettle by its wire handle. She tried to lift it, but it wouldn't budge. She tugged at it. It seemed to be fastened to the hearth. Maybe this was Mrs. Bell's idea of a joke.

Mrs. Bell turned around. "Oh, can't you lift it, dear?" She came to the hearth and lifted the kettle easily off the floor. "I just wasn't thinking about how heavy this old thing is," she said as she carried the kettle outside.

So that was it. She was trying to make Molly look weak. Angrily, Molly stormed through the door after her. Behind Molly, Rachel came down the steps one by one, into the yard.

Arabella was holding a pointed piece of hard soap that looked like a peeled parsnip. With an iron knife, she shaved off a few curls that fell pinging into a tin basin on the washing table. "Pour in some hot water, Molly," she said.

Molly already knew she couldn't lift the kettle, and Mrs. Bell had returned to the house. So Molly just stood there with her arms folded and glared angrily at Arabella. Out of the corner of her eye, she noticed that Rachel had folded her arms too, and was trying to match her glare. Arabella shrugged and picked up the kettle, sloshing some water into the basin.

"Now take this whisk and stir it up."

Molly took the bundle of straw Arabella handled her and made a few dispirited swipes at the water.

"Faster," said Arabella.

Molly beat angrily at the water, churning it into a thick foam of soapsuds that glinted with rainbow colors in the afternoon sunlight. Molly couldn't help but smile.

"Yes, it's nice, isn't it?" said Arabella. "Now put the dishes in."

Molly quickly turned her accidental smile into a scowl. Nobody had done anything but tell her what to do since she'd landed, and it seemed like this was going to go on forever. "They've still got food stuck to 'em," she said.

"They won't once we wash them," said Arabella with exaggerated patience.

"That's a waste of food," said Molly. "We should just let it dry on the plates and then . . ."

Arabella looked queasy. "Yes, well, we're not going to. Now put the dishes in. Come on, like this." She picked up a wooden plate and dropped it into the suds. "No, not that one!"

Molly put down the clay plate she was holding. "Make up your bleedin' mind, then."

"That's a meat dish. These are dairy dishes. Dishes for meat have to be kept separate from dishes for anything made with milk."

"That's stupid." Molly folded her arms again, and Rachel hastily imitated her.

Arabella pursed her lips. "Well, try and remember it, anyway. Separate dishes, separate pots, and separate knives for meat and cheese. That's kosher."

Molly backed away. Arabella could wash the dishes herself if she was going to be so bleedin' picky. "We don't wash dishes in Seven Dials."

"Uh-huh. Well, you're here now. Try and make the best of it." Arabella went on picking up dishes and placing them in the water. "If you're not going to help with the dishes, go get me some cold water."

Molly didn't move: she had no intention of following orders and doing stupid work that didn't need doing. She stayed there with her arms folded. Arabella ignored her, so Molly sat down on the flagstones to make it clear that she wasn't going to do what anyone told her to. Rachel sat down next to her, checking to make sure that she had her legs crossed like Molly's. Molly looked away from her in annoyance.

"Fine! I'll go get the water," Arabella snapped, putting down a plate and the rag she'd been scrubbing it with. "You should be grateful that the Bells have fed you and put clothes on your back, but all you've managed to do so far is spill the bathwater and make dinner late."

She shook suds from her hands, dried them on her apron, and went back into the house.

Molly felt tears start in her eyes, which made her even angrier because she didn't even care what stupid people like Arabella thought of her. Certainly not enough to cry. She jumped up and ran through the wooden gate of the kitchen yard, letting the stone weight pull it closed behind her with a bang. A moment later, it banged again, but she didn't look back. Tears blurring her eyes, she lurched out into the street and stumbled back the way she had come with Mr. Bell. Arabella hated her, Mr. and Mrs. Bell hated her, and she hated them. She should have told Captain Mattock she wouldn't go with Mr. Bell. Maybe it wasn't too late.

Wiping her eyes angrily on her blue woolen sleeve, she turned down Broad Street. The tears kept dripping from her eyes, and people stared. She saw a woman in wooden shoes and a winged white hat leading a goat by a rope, and an African boy yelling at a donkey that had stopped in the middle of the street and refused to budge. She saw a man dressed like a London dandy in a bottle-green velvet coat, a wig of pinkish white curls, and a sword swinging from his belt. A man dressed in buckskins, his red hair greased back into a club, was standing in the street, looking around as if he'd just arrived from another world.

The street was wide and quiet, and the locust and ironwood trees growing down the middle of it made it look more like a field than like any street in London. Birds chirped loudly in the tree branches. There were no carriages or wagons, and none of the people seemed to have anything more interesting to look at or think about than Molly.

The woman with the wooden shoes came up to Molly and put a hand on her head, saying something gently in what Molly thought was Dutch. The goat rubbed the top of its head against Molly's leg. Molly angrily pushed past the woman and the goat and went down to the dock, where she had landed that morning.

The docks were noisy and busy. Men in striped shirts and wide trousers were rolling barrels from ships, and a market full of men and women arguing in several languages was spread out on the cobbles. The docks smelled of rotten fruit, fish, and the sea.

The *Good Intention* was still docked at the pier. Molly saw Captain Mattock and his first mate sitting on an overturned handcart on the dock, sorting through the pile of indentures.

Molly sniffed and managed to stop crying. "Captain Mattock!"

He turned around and looked at her. There was no sign of recognition in his eyes.

But the mate recognized her. "It's Mary Abraham," he said, smiling. "How does New York suit you, Mary?"

"It doesn't," said Molly, trying to control the tears that threatened to start up again. "I hate it, and I want to go back. I've changed my mind about being sold to Mr. Bell."

"Oh, I remember you now," said Captain Mattock. "The little Jewess."

"You have to be sold to someone, Mary," said the mate.

"And Bell's paid for you," Captain Mattock added. "We've just taken the last of his wheat aboard, and we're on our way to register your indenture now."

"Those Bells are good folk," the mate said. "I've been to their shop many times."

"They are that." Captain Mattock shrugged. "I may not be good folk, but I know 'em when I see 'em. They'll see you turn out right."

"I don't want to turn out right," said Molly angrily. "I want to go home."

Captain Mattock sneered. "It's four pounds for the fare to London. And even if you've got it, you'll still end up riding a horse foaled by an acorn."

Molly knew that was one of the hundreds of ways to say "hanged" in London slang. "Couldn't you sell me again? Like you sold me to Mr. Bell? Only in England?"

Captain Mattock shook his head. "You belong to Bell now, until you reach the age of twenty-one. He paid for you. That's the law."

"But, I mean, I'll work twice as long." Molly said this with a hard swallow, because she didn't want to belong to anybody or do their work. "All the time I'm supposed to work for the Bells, and all that time again to pay for going back to England."

Captain Mattock shook his head. "Can't be done. It only works one way. In America there's lots of work to be done and not enough people to do it. In England, there's whatcha call a 'surplus population.'" He uttered the last two words slowly, as though measuring them with his tongue. "Too many people and no work for them to do. You ain't worth a tin shilling in London."

Molly thought about that for a minute. "Well, if I can get four pounds? Could you take me then?"

"Still can't do it. You belong to Bell. And he's your own kind, so you oughta stick with 'im."

Molly looked helplessly at the mate. He shook his head at her with a smile.

"You better listen to me, as knows," said Captain Mattock. "You'd have gone from picking pockets on hanging days at Tyburn to swinging from Tyburn Tree yourself. I've seen enough do so in my time. So you stick with what you've got and be grateful for it. Understand?"

Molly felt the tears starting again. The mate held out a handkerchief, and she looked at it in confusion.

"It's to blow your nose on, not to sell," said Captain Mattock sarcastically. "Now, get yourself back to the Bells where you belong, and take the baby with you."

Molly suddenly became aware of something tugging at her skirt—Mrs. Bell's cut-down skirt—and looked down to see Rachel standing beside her.

"Pick up me," said Rachel.

"Yes, pick up her," Captain Mattock agreed. "Take her home, go home, grow up decent, and don't hang." He turned his back on her.

The mate smiled at Molly again, encouragingly, and patted her on the shoulder with a grimy hand. Wordlessly, Molly handed back the handkerchief. She hadn't used it, because she didn't want to get it dirty. Those things were worth money. The mate meant well, but neither the mate nor the captain was going to help her at all. Talking to each other and thumbing through their pile of indentures, they wandered off together through the market.

"Up!" Rachel demanded, lifting her arms toward Molly.

Molly bent down and lifted Rachel. She wasn't as heavy as the kettle of water, but she was heavy. Molly balanced her awkwardly on her hip, as she had seen other girls do. She had never carried a baby before, and she thought Rachel was too big to carry. She looked up at the deck of the *Good Intention*. There seemed to be no one on it. Just the prisoners who hadn't been sold, she guessed, locked up in the hold. Rachel wrapped her arms around Molly's neck, and Molly turned around and went back to Mill Street.

After months of sleeping on the damp, curving boards of the ship, bracing her body against the rolling sea, Molly found it hard to lie still next to Arabella in the cabinet bed. It seemed ridiculously luxurious to have a whole straw mattress long enough for a mort to stretch out on, and the sheets and blankets were stifling. Besides, she had never slept on a nib lig like this, up off the floor. Molly kept turning over between Arabella and the wall, onto one side and then the other.

"Would you stop?" said Arabella.

"I can't sleep."

"Well, I could if someone would let me. Count something. Or recite something."

Molly didn't know anything to recite, and she couldn't think of anything to count. "Who's that Mrs. Grip woman?" she asked.

"An old piece of misery," said Arabella. "Don't pay attention to anything she says. Nobody does."

"Who was that Moses cove she was talking about?"

Arabella sighed. "A convict, out of London. Nothing to do with you."

"What did he do?"

"Stole some gold. And was hanged."

Molly pondered this in silence for a moment. "They hang people in New York?"

"Aren't you ever going to be still?"

"And he was Jewish? Is Mrs. Grip Jewish?"

Arabella didn't answer. But Molly didn't want to stop talking now. She didn't want to be left alone with her thoughts in the dark, so far from London.

"Are you Jewish, Arabella?"

Arabella let out a chuckle and propped herself up on her elbows. "For Pete's sake, child. Do I look Jewish?"

"I don't know. Why do you live with the Bells, then?"

"Because they own me," said Arabella. She lay back down.

"Like me, you mean?"

"No, not like you. For life. I'm a slave. And a very tired one. Now be quiet."

Molly hadn't known it was possible to be a slave for life. "What did they snabble you for?" she asked. And then, when Arabella didn't answer, she added, "Arrest you for, I mean."

"For being born with this black skin," said Arabella. "If you don't be quiet now, I'm going to make you sleep on the floor."

Molly tried to keep still and make herself go to sleep, but it wasn't possible. She thought about what

Arabella had said. Molly had known a few people in London with black skin—a woman called Black Joan and two men who were both called Othello. But they weren't slaves. Molly didn't think she'd ever known a slave in London.

The rules in this remote, strange country were different, and, just as she'd feared, she didn't understand them.

Six

It wasn't until late the next day that Molly got a chance to look around the house. It was small, but it was the fanciest Molly had ever been in—a real bob-ken. It had four rooms, and there were no other families in the house to share them with. On the ground floor was the kitchen and a front room. The front room had a painted floorcloth made from old sail canvas, benches, a table, and a shelf full of books. The spiral staircase made Molly nervous at first, because in Molly's experience staircases tended to collapse. But it didn't tremble and barely creaked when she climbed it. Upstairs was where Mr. and Mrs. Bell, David, and Rachel slept. Molly had heard them getting up in the morning and praying, mostly David and Mr. Bell. Then David and Mr. Bell had gone off to the synagogue and Mrs. Bell had come downstairs and given Molly chores to do.

After the midday dinner, Molly went into the front

room and looked at the books on the shelves. She had already looked at almost everything else in the house. Mr. Bell walked in while she was flipping through one of them, and she dropped it in fright.

"That's Hebrew," said Mr. Bell, picking the book up carefully. "If you were a boy, you'd learn to read Hebrew. But we want you to learn to read English, Molly."

"I'm not no jarkman," said Molly.

"You don't have to be a forger to learn to read," said Mr. Bell. "There are other uses for reading and writing besides forgery, you know."

Molly looked at him askance. "You patter Flash?"

"A little bit," he said, smiling. "I told you, I'm from London too."

Molly edged away from him and left the room. Everyone from London did not speak Flash-cant, or understand it. That was the whole point of speaking Flash—so nib culls wouldn't understand you. She wondered if Mr. Bell was quite the nib cull he seemed.

Reading was important to the Bells. In the months that followed, Molly ended up learning to read because she got tired of resisting. It didn't make much difference since she wasn't planning to stay, and anyway, she might be able to learn enough to be a jarkman when she got back to London. Arabella and Mrs. Bell taught her to make letters with her finger on a pile of sand on the table in the front room, while Mr. Bell and David studied from Hebrew books taken from the corner shelf. David wore his three-cornered hat, and Mr. Bell wore a bright green turban that covered the short brown hair that stuck out every which way when he took off his wig. Mrs. Bell told her that men and boys always covered their heads when they prayed or when they read holy books.

After Molly learned the letters, she started learning the words in *The English Spelling Book*. Sometimes Mrs. Bell taught her, and sometimes Arabella did. Arabella had learned to read when she was little, at a school for slaves kept by a Frenchman named Mr. Neau.

Besides teaching Molly to read, Mrs. Bell made her learn to darn with a bone needle. Weaving yarn over the holes in her gray stockings was easy. Molly had been trained to pick pockets since before she could remember, and her fingers were used to quick, complicated movements.

"You have the makings of a fine needlewoman, Molly," said Mrs. Bell approvingly, and Molly smiled cautiously. At least she was keeping her fingers nimble for when she got back to London.

The whole family made her nervous. David hadn't done anything to her yet, but that was probably because his parents were always around. Rachel clung to Molly's skirts all the time and followed her whenever she went outside, making it impossible for Molly to go very far or to see much of New York on her own. Arabella, Molly had discovered, always insisted on sleeping on the outside of their bed, as if she expected Molly might try to escape during the night. But Molly wasn't ready to escape just yet. She needed a plan. What she wanted to do was to get outside in the dark so that she could see what New York was really like.

But every night, Molly fell into bed and went right to sleep, exhausted. Mrs. Bell thought of things for her to do all day long. Besides washing the dishes, which they did every single time they used them, there were

turnips to scrub and cut up, and peas to pick through. There was meat from the shochet, the kosher butcher, that had to be soaked in salt and then in water before it could be cooked. There was more water to haul, because Mrs. Bell never seemed to tire of cleaning things. Mrs. Bell and Arabella and Molly even cleaned the family's scowring-cheats—every shirt and stocking. There was wood to carry in to make up the fires. Every time Molly thought she was finished and could slip off on her own for a while, Mrs. Bell would take her by the arm and call her "dear" and give her something else to do.

Mr. Bell was frightening. It wasn't just that he knew Flash, which no nib cull in a powdered wig ought to know, but also that he had loud friends. In the evening, while the women sewed or read, men would stop by to visit and talk with Mr. Bell and David. Mostly they talked in the language Molly didn't know, Yiddish, but they would switch to English in the middle of a sentence. The talking would turn into arguing, and Molly kept waiting for the fighting to start and the knives to come out, but so far the men had only fought with books. They pulled books down from the shelves and flipped through them, laying them open on the table and crying out happily when they found words to support their arguments. They seemed to have a wonderful time with this, and Mrs. Bell and Arabella would smile at them and shake their heads. But Molly found it nerve-wracking.

Women came to visit too. They came in through the kitchen door during the day, sometimes borrowing something and sometimes bringing something—fresh butter, or peas from their gardens, or cowslip wine, or kosher soap. They all looked at Molly with great curiosity. Some of them spoke to her very slowly, as if they thought she might not be very bright. Molly tried not to let it bother her. Sometimes it could be useful to have people think you were stupid.

Molly saw the women again on the days that she went to the synagogue. Mr. Bell and David went to the synagogue every morning and every evening. Sometimes they stayed there for prayers; sometimes they came back right away. Molly learned that there had to be a minyan, which meant ten men, to say prayers. If there weren't ten men at the synagogue, Mr. Bell and David would say their prayers in the parlor together.

On Saturday mornings, Mrs. Bell and Molly and little Rachel went to the synagogue as well. It was a brand-new brick building on Mill Street, near the Bells' house. David and Mr. Bell went in through the main door, and Mrs. Bell led Molly and Rachel up a staircase on the side of the building to the women's gallery.

The gallery wrapped around three sides of the building. If you sat on the bench against the wall, you couldn't see over the railing, but if you went to the railing and looked through the latticework, you could see the men gathered below. Molly listened to them talking, saying prayers, and reading from a Torah scroll.

It was a bit like being in a cage, Molly thought, as she looked down one Saturday morning at the tops of the men's hats. It was hard to pick out Mr. Bell—one three-cornered hat and powdered wig among a roomful of hats and wigs—but easier to find David, whose curly brown hair was tied back at his neck with a ribbon. Mrs. Bell could never get him to powder his hair because, he said, the powder made him itch and sneeze.

The women in the balcony talked to each other in English and Yiddish, and in other languages that Molly gradually found out were German, Spanish, Portuguese, and Ladino. Mrs. Bell seemed to understand all of these languages, and to speak them. When Molly asked her, she said that Portuguese was her native language.

"I learned Yiddish when I met Mr. Bell, and then a few other languages as I went along," she said with a smile.

A lot of the gossiping women were talking about Molly. Especially the ones who gathered around Adah Grip. She could tell by the way they looked at her.

One day she heard Mrs. Grip say, in plain English, "I can't understand why the Bells would do it—take in a common criminal from the London streets, a convict who's done who-knows-what nasty crimes, and bring her into the house to mingle with their own children."

Her insides boiling, Molly turned around, looked at Mrs. Grip, and forced herself to smile. Not because she felt like smiling, but to show the stupid woman that nothing she said could hurt her. The smile didn't work very well, though. The corners of Molly's mouth kept twitching and jumping, and Mrs. Grip wasn't impressed.

"It's a mitzvah, a good deed, to take them in," one of the women next to Mrs. Grip said under her breath. Or at least that's what Molly thought she said, because the woman spoke in Yiddish.

Mrs. Grip answered back, something in Yiddish that Molly couldn't understand but which sounded extremely nasty.

Little bits of Yiddish were beginning to make sense to Molly. The Bells spoke it at home sometimes, although they spoke English too. And Molly had a vague memory of her mother speaking Yiddish a long time ago. Not to her, but to somebody else. A man, Molly thought, but not one of the men friends who came and went later. A man whose lap Molly had sat on. And not in the room in Seven Dials that she remembered. Somewhere else. The rest of the memory wouldn't come.

It was quite clear to Molly that the Bells hadn't bought her as a mitzvah, if that meant a good deed. She was doing a lot of hard work for them, more work than she'd done in her whole life up till now. And they kept finding more for her to do. If that was their idea of a good deed, they were making the most of it.

"Well, they say the mother was Jewish," said Adah Grip, speaking English again, and loudly. "But you can imagine the sort of woman she must have been."

Molly spun around angrily, ready to tell Adah Grip and everyone else in the synagogue exactly what sort of woman Mrs. Grip was. Mrs. Bell grabbed Molly's arm and pulled her back, frowning at Mrs. Grip and her gossips at the same time. But it wasn't the kind of frown that was likely to shut them up. There was no venom in it, Molly thought angrily. Mrs. Bell didn't know how to fight. She drew Molly and Rachel farther down the synagogue gallery, away from Adah Grip's cronies.

Molly shrugged off Mrs. Bell's grasp and went to the railing. She looked through the latticework at the men down below. They had all risen to their feet, and Molly heard the women on the bench behind her standing up. A man Molly didn't know went to a pair of doors in the wall below and opened them. Molly saw several tall bundles covered in silk, with silver crowns on top of them.

"What *are* those?" she asked Mrs. Bell.

"The Torah scrolls. Don't point, dear," said Mrs. Bell.

"What *are* they?"

"Holy books. They tell us the law that was given to our people Israel, and written down by Moses."

"You mean the cove that was scragged for filching some gold?" said Molly, remembering the thief Arabella had told her about. "Moses What's-his-face?"

Mrs. Bell frowned. "Molly, what on earth are you talking about?"

Molly turned away in embarrassment, because she had just remembered that there was another cove named Moses who had wandered in the desert for forty years and received the mitzvoth, the commandments, from God. Mrs. Bell had told her about him before.

Molly watched a man carrying a scroll from the ark to the reading desk in the middle of the room below. The scroll was rolled onto two wooden poles and was covered with a breastplate that Molly recognized as real silver. Two silver ornaments topped the poles. Molly squinted and leaned forward, trying to see them better. The were conical, like sugarloaves, and each had what looked like a silver crown on top. There were some finer details that Molly's blurry vision couldn't make out. The scroll jingled as it moved, though, so she guessed there must be small silver bells attached to the cones.

"What about them jingle-box things on top?" asked Molly, pressing her forehead against the wooden lattice as she tried to get a closer look.

"Those are the rimonim," said Mrs. Bell. "You can recognize the different scrolls by them. 'Rimonim' means 'pomegranates.' I don't know why they call them that. A pomegranate is a fruit we used to eat in Barbados when I was a girl. The hazzan keeps changing scrolls to make sure that every scroll gets used." The expression in her eyes seemed far away, the way it sometimes did . . . far away in Barbados, perhaps. Wherever that was.

"Why does every scroll have to get used?" asked Molly.

"Different families gave the scrolls, and they all want their scrolls to be used."

"Is that the hazzan?" Molly asked, pointing to the man at the reading desk in the middle of the room. Molly could see his hat, the back of his wig, and his prayer shawl, but not his face.

"Don't point, dear. Yes, he's the hazzan, Mr. de

Fonseca. In Europe, there'd be a rabbi too, but . . ." She shrugged.

"But what?" said Molly.

"None of the rabbis want to come to America," a woman nearby said. "Rabbis are men of learning, and they like to be around other men of learning. So we have a hazzan instead."

"I didn't want to come to America either," said Adah Grip, who had followed them, probably so she could keep annoying them. "But nobody asked me, and here I am."

Mrs. Bell was still wearing her faraway look. She smiled at Adah in a distracted way. Molly wondered if Mrs. Bell had wanted to come to America.

Rachel tugged at Molly's skirt. "Take me to the privy."

Mrs. Bell looked relieved. "Take her outside, Molly, won't you?"

"I wouldn't be surprised if the Bells woke up one morning to find they'd been murdered in their sleep," Adah said to someone as Molly took Rachel by the hand and started to leave the gallery. "Then they'll wish they'd listened to me."

Murdered? Molly scowled. There was a big difference between being a pickpocket (a good one) and being a bleedin' murderer. She managed to step on the hem of Adah's gown as she pushed past her. Molly wished her feet were muddy.

The sun was shining brightly. Birds were circling low, chirping loudly. Molly led Rachel toward the little outhouse behind the synagogue.

Rachel dug her heels in. "I want to go to *my* privy," she said.

"Your privy?" said Molly.

"My at-home privy."

They walked home, and Molly waited while Rachel used the little wooden privy behind the Bells' house. Soon Rachel came out, banging the door shut behind her.

"I want to go to the market," she said.

"We can't go to the market," said Molly. "It's the Sabbath. We're supposed to go back to the synagogue. Come on."

Since most New Yorkers were Christians, Saturday was a market day. But for Jews it was the Sabbath, and they weren't supposed to do any kind of work at all. That was fine with Molly, who was heartily sick of work. But according to the Bells, "work" included all sorts of things—not just starting the kitchen fire and cooking, but things like lighting a candle or walking around town.

"That's why we'd be lost without Arabella," Mrs. Bell often said, smiling. Since Arabella was a Christian, she could do all the things that the Bells and Molly weren't supposed to do on the Sabbath.

Molly was sure that walking down to the market by

the docks was something Jews weren't supposed to do on the Sabbath. Although it seemed far preferable to going back into the synagogue, with Adah Grip there.

"I want to go to the market," said Rachel. She stamped her foot.

Molly thought about it. She would rather go to the market too. She hadn't yet had a chance to explore it properly. She'd only been there with Mrs. Bell, following her with a basket while Mrs. Bell argued the price of turnips with the farmers from Harlem and Long Island.

But Mrs. Bell would be expecting them back at the synagogue. "Some other time," said Molly regretfully. "Now come along."

She reached down for Rachel's hand. Rachel clenched her hands into tiny fists and stamped her foot. "I want to go to the market-market-market! I want to see my sweetheart man!"

Molly couldn't resist smiling at the way Rachel made up names for people. The sweetheart man was an old Huguenot Frenchman who sold goods to peddlers. The peddlers bought ribbons and buttons, needles and pins, from him and stowed them away in big metal cans they carried on their shoulders as they walked into the countryside. The farther they got from Manhattan, the higher the prices they could charge for the goods they had bought from the old Frenchman in the market.

The Frenchman always called Rachel his sweetheart, and sometimes he gave her a bit of ribbon from his stock. Mrs. Bell had tried to pay him for the gifts, but he'd said, "I may be a poor man, madame, but you'll make me a much poorer one if you don't let me give something to my little sweetheart now and then." Mrs. Bell could see that this was true, so she contented herself with teaching Rachel to curtsey and say, "Thank you, sir."

"We'll see your sweetheart man soon," said Molly. "Right now we have to go back to the synagogue."

"Boring synagogue!" said Rachel.

Molly privately agreed. The Sabbath service would go on for hours, and Molly would much rather be out exploring New York. But Mrs. Bell would be expecting them back. Molly reached down, grabbed Rachel's arm, and started pulling her toward the synagogue.

Rachel broke free and ran down Mill Street, toward the river. Molly chased after her. Rachel was fast for such a little girl, but her legs were short. Molly caught her by the back of her smock when she had reached the corner.

Rachel twisted in Molly's grip and started to scream. Molly felt like screaming herself. Why couldn't you reason with the kinchin? But Molly really didn't want to go back to the synagogue either. It was much nicer outside, and unlike the women in the gallery, Rachel actually seemed to like Molly.

And Molly did want a chance to get a closer look at the market.

"All right," she said. "We will go to the market and we will see your sweetheart man. And then we will go back to the synagogue, and you won't blow the gab to nobody. You surtoute what I'm saying?"

Rachel brightened. "Yes!"

Molly took Rachel's hand and trudged down the street beside the East River, the little girl skipping at her side.

Suddenly Rachel stopped. "Tie my bonnet," she instructed Molly. Exasperated, Molly knelt on the dusty street. She could tell from the sound of drunken laughter that they were in front of a boozing-ken.

It was an old wooden shack that looked as if it had been thrown together from scraps left over from someone else's house. There was only one small square window, and it had no glass. The door hung open on leather hinges. A dead bush nailed over the door identified it as an inn, but Molly would have known that anyway from the sour smell of rum mixed with the odor of people not bothering to go outside to use the privy. From inside came voices, slurred and muttering, then more loud laughter. Someone cursed angrily and then began to sob.

Molly stood up and stared into the inn's doorway. The people inside were dark shapes moving in the shadows. If she had been in London, she would have gone in, looking for something to eat or a fencing cull to buy something she'd managed to nip. She felt Rachel's small, sticky hand tug at her own.

Hesper Crudge stepped out of the dark room, squinting in the sunlight. She and Molly froze and stared at each other in surprise. Molly hadn't seen Hesper since she had left the ship. She hadn't even known that Hesper was still in New York.

Hesper was dirtier than anyone Molly had seen in a long time, and she was still wearing Molly's clogs. Her bedraggled, colorless dress hung over a body that was skinnier than Molly remembered. Even the sly, feral grin on her cutthroat's face had a starveling look to it.

Hesper was sizing Molly up too, and still grinning. "I see you have new stamper cases," she said.

"Yes," said Molly. She looked down at the buckskin moccasins that the Bells had had made especially for her. Then she looked at her old clogs on Hesper's feet. The leather tops were soaking wet. Hesper's feet were bigger than Molly's, and her heels stuck out over the ends of the wooden soles. She still didn't have any stockings, and her feet looked red and sore.

For some reason, Molly's own feet suddenly felt itchy and too warm in her dry, comfortable moccasins.

Just then a man and a woman lurched out of the doorway arm in arm and knocked into Hesper. Hesper fell against Molly, and Molly jumped back.

"Oh, did I get your nice clean clothes dirty?" said Hesper, smirking as she righted herself. "You'd better run home and take a bath, hadn't you?"

Rachel tugged on Molly's hand. "Carry me!" she demanded.

Molly bent down, grasped Rachel under the arms, and swung her up onto her hip. She had an uncomfortable prickling feeling in her chest. She was horribly afraid she might be feeling sorry for Hesper Crudge. She turned on her heel and walked away without another word.

It wasn't far to the harbor. The wide, cobbled pavement beside the docks was crowded with sailors and porters, people rolling barrels and hauling crates to be loaded onto ships, sailors unloading cargo with ropes and pulleys, and amid it all, market stalls and vendors calling out their wares in Dutch and English. Molly could smell onions and cabbages, and the hot oil used to fry the sugar-topped cakes called dough-knots that the Dutch farmers sold.

In London, the smell of food cooking in a market used to draw Molly toward it, as if she had no will of her own. She remembered how the vendors would watch her sharply, ready to chase her off if they saw her come too close to their wares.

A London pie-woman had once given her a steak-and-kidney pie for nothing. Not a burnt pie or a broken one either, but a perfectly good one. The woman had even jabbed a hole in the top with her thumb and poured in a ladleful of hot gravy. Molly had seized the steaming pie and run away, afraid the pie-woman might change her mind. Then she'd hidden in an alley and wolfed it down, too hungry to savor the hot, salty gravy.

Now, in the market on the docks in New York, Molly breathed in the smell of fish. She remembered how simple and countrified New York had looked to her the day she arrived. Now this scene beside the docks seemed chaotic. And on the Sabbath too. She thought that London was like this all over, all the time. That wasn't possible, was it?

"Where's my sweetheart man?" Rachel said loudly. Several people standing nearby looked at the little girl in surprise and laughed.

"You've got your hands full with that one, missy," a man said to Molly.

Molly looked around. She didn't know where the ribbon-and-button man was. She thought that he always set up close to the docks where the ships were moored. But she and Rachel had worked their way through the crowd to the docks and he wasn't there.

A small crowd had gathered at the end of the market, where a ship's prow loomed overhead like a great bare tree branch. It wouldn't have counted as a crowd in London—it was just a few dozen people. With Rachel clinging to her skirts, Molly pushed her way forward, weaving her way expertly to the front of the crowd. A cove in a farmer's smock was having his tooth pulled. He lay flat on his back on a small platform, his head gripped between the knees of the tooth-puller, who was leaning over him, a long-handled pair of forceps gripped in both hands. The tooth-puller was tugging with all his might. Sweat stood out in little droplets on both men's faces. Molly's eyes traveled automatically to the patient's pockets. There was something in one of them—a purse, maybe. The audience was watching. But maybe in a few minutes, at the moment the tooth came out, they would be distracted. . . .

Molly looked at the patient's face again. She saw tears sliding from the corners of his eyes, running down into his ears. She had a sudden flash of what it must feel like to have an aching tooth gripped in forged-iron pliers and jerked about by a sweaty-smelling tooth-puller on a stage with a plaguey lot of strangers watching. She shuddered.

Then Molly noticed a woman sliding around the edge of the platform, as if trying to get a closer look at the tooth-puller. The woman was really getting as close as possible to the pocket with the bulge in it, in order to make her grab quickly when the tooth came out. She looked almost like Mrs. Wilkes, only a little cleaner. Could she actually *be* Mrs. Wilkes? Molly wanted to call out her name, but now would be a bad time. She didn't want to ruin the woman's filch.

Rachel tugged at Molly's skirts. "I want my sweetheart man!"

Molly looked down at Rachel. She couldn't pick the

cove's pocket with Rachel clinging to her skirt, anyway. "He's not here. Let's go," she said. She led Rachel back through the crowd.

"I want my—"

"He's not here," Molly told Rachel again. "Maybe he's looking for more ribbons to sell."

"I want my sweetheart man!" said Rachel.

A ship's captain in high-topped leather boots stopped and stooped down to look at Rachel. "Of course you do, little one. And shall I be your sweetheart man?"

Rachel shook her head and ducked behind Molly.

The captain looked at Molly. "And what are two such lovely ladies doing on the docks unattended? Are you looking for passage on a ship?"

Molly drew a sharp breath. "Do you go to England?"

The captain smiled. "Ofttimes I do. Would you be wanting to work your passage to England?"

"Oh, yes," Molly breathed, taking a step forward so Rachel wouldn't hear her. Then she took another look at the captain. He wore a purple velvet coat, with dozens of gold buttons, and a diamond brooch. His sweeping black beaver hat had three pink ostrich plumes on it. It was a nib outfit for a working ship's master.

"Then I'm sure I can find space for you sometime or another," said the captain. "I'm René Duguay, and my ship's the *Revenge*. Care to come aboard and look around?"

"N-no," said Molly, taking two steps backward. Her

London instincts told her that René Duguay was a flash-cove if ever she'd met one. And a dangerous one. Still, if he could get her back to London . . . "Well, maybe later. Right now I've got to look after the baby." She reached down to pat Rachel on the head.

But Rachel wasn't there.

Molly turned and looked quickly around. She saw the jumble of market stalls and the crowds of shoppers poking at the goods and arguing with the sellers. She even saw Hesper Crudge, carrying a basket and following a fat woman. She saw a broken melon on the cobbles, and an African woman and an Englishman arguing angrily about who had dropped it.

But there was no Rachel to be seen.

Seven

Molly felt a surge of panic in her stomach, and her face was burning. She tried to call Rachel's name, but no sound came out of her mouth. She tried again, and only coughed. Finally, she cried, "Rachel! Rachel!" but her voice sounded weak and strange. It seemed that nobody was paying any attention.

"There, love." Mrs. Wilkes was suddenly by her side.

Molly had never been so glad to see anyone in her life.

So it *had* been Mrs. Wilkes she'd seen trying to pick that cove's pocket—but there was no time to think about that now. "I lost Rachel. Mrs. Wilkes, help me. I'll be frummagemmed by the Bells."

"Now, dear. What's lost can be found. Who's Rachel, and where did you lose her?"

Molly described Rachel, and in an instant Mrs.

Wilkes had appropriated a packing crate and had climbed up on top of it to survey the crowd.

"I don't see your Rachel, love. Let me call." And then, to Molly's astonished embarrassment, Mrs. Wilkes yelled to the crowd, *"We've lost a little girl!!"*

"How little?" a woman shouted.

And Mrs. Wilkes called out a description of Rachel, from her curly yellow hair to her sky-blue smock. Everybody within earshot began looking about, but soon people shrugged and went back about their business. A young African woman whom Molly recognized as Christy, a friend of Arabella's, pushed her way out of the crowd and stood before Molly and Mrs. Wilkes. "You've lost Rachel?" said Christy. "Let me help you look for her."

"Good. We must try the water first," said Mrs. Wilkes. "You two girls run along the water's edge and look all over in the river."

"The . . . the river?" Molly echoed. She suddenly felt as if a hangman's noose were tightening around her guts.

"Yes, at once. And I'll go get those people of yours to help. Where are they?"

"They're in the synagogue," said Molly. "But don't . . ." She was terrified of what the Bells would say. "They're not allowed to do anything on Saturdays," she said, "so they can't help us look."

"Nonsense!" said Mrs. Wilkes briskly. "Now, you get down along the water there and look, and quickly."

Christy was already running along the dock, looking into the water. Mrs. Wilkes gave Molly a shove in the direction of the dockside, and Molly ran along the quay, stopping every few feet to look down between the wooden moorings, into the river and to call Rachel's name. She couldn't see very far into the water. Would a little girl sink or float? Why hadn't she just dragged the wretched child back to the synagogue?

The harbor was divided into two great squares of water, the East Dock and the West Dock, by a narrow quay that ran out from the market to the East River. Molly ran along the whole of the East Dock, peering into the narrow crack between shipside and quayside, and was starting around the West Dock when a crowd of people came running up, surrounding her.

It seemed that every Jew in New York had come running from the synagogue together. All of the women, and all of the men, and all of the children. Everyone was talking at once: "Where did you see her last?" "Where did you lose her?"

And other people were yelling too, in Spanish and Portuguese and Ladino and Yiddish and Dutch and German, poking at people in front of them and demanding translations.

Molly pointed to the area by the market where she'd last seen Rachel, and in a few moments the mob had broken up into search parties, some combing the dock-sides, some going through the market, some questioning sailors and stevedores along the quays. David and another boy got into a small boat and began poling along the dock, searching the water.

Molly was hoping that the Bells had forgotten about her, but Mrs. Bell caught her firmly by the arm. "Show me exactly where you saw her last," she said. "Come on; take me to the very spot."

Mrs. Bell's voice was quiet, but her face was drawn and white. It was frightening to look at her. Wordlessly, Molly led her to where she had been standing when she was speaking to René Duguay. They had to dodge their way past hundreds of people, all looking for Rachel. The arrival of all the Jews together had finally alerted the sellers and shoppers in the market to the gravity of the situation. Everyone joined in the search, pushing and shoving each other in their haste.

"What on earth possessed you to bring her down here?" asked Mrs. Bell tightly.

"She said she wanted to find her sweetheart man," Molly said.

"Sweetheart . . . ?"

"The man who sells ribbons." Molly was surprised Mrs. Bell didn't know. "I thought people weren't sup-posed to run around like this on the Sabbath," she added.

"Nonsense!" snapped Mrs. Bell, just like Mrs.

Wilkes. "God can wait. People can't. Where does that ribbon man usually set up?"

So they looked for the ribbon man, although Molly was quite sure by now that he wasn't there. In fact, none of the sellers were at their stalls anymore; they were all running around looking for Rachel. Molly noticed Hesper Crudge again, eyeing the unattended stalls with interest. It was a perfect opportunity for a pickpocket. But Molly wasn't even tempted. All she wanted was to find Rachel.

Molly looked around. The crowd of searchers was concentrating more and more around the water's edge. Mrs. Bell noticed this too. She clenched Molly's arm so tightly it hurt. Her hands were shaking.

Then, from the crow's nest of one of the ships, a sailor called out, "Ahoy!"

On the deck, another sailor held aloft a tiny figure in a sky-blue smock.

The whole crowd surged down the quay toward the ship, and in the rush three people got knocked into the water. But no harm done, Mrs. Wilkes assured Molly. Rachel was smothered with hugs and kisses and demands to know what had possessed her to go climbing aboard a ship, for goodness' sake.

Nobody gave Rachel a chance to answer, but Molly was sure Rachel had been looking for her sweetheart man.

Molly hung back as the other Jews returned to the

synagogue. She couldn't face Mrs. Bell, or Mr. Bell, or anybody. She even thought momentarily of going with that René Duguay cove, but he had vanished utterly during the search for Rachel.

"Chin up, ducks," said Mrs. Wilkes. "It's only a whipping, and soon over."

Molly nodded distractedly. There wasn't going to be any whipping at the Bells', because she wasn't going back.

Eight

Molly found it easy to get separated from the Bells in the crowded market. Crowds were something she knew. She walked up Broadway, avoiding the Jews returning to the synagogue. And she kept walking. She passed the pillory and the whipping post in front of the city hall. She followed the road past the rope walk, and the pottery kilns, and the Collect Pond, and the windmill. The road became a track, leading through woodlands and fields and past the occasional farmhouses that dotted the Manhattan countryside. A breeze blowing across a field brought a scent of hydrangeas with it.

Rachel could easily have drowned, Molly thought. And it would have been Molly's fault. Just because Molly hadn't felt like going back to the synagogue and listening to Adah Grip and her gossips talk about what an unchancy mitzvah Molly was! And Adah Grip was right. Molly didn't belong in the Bells' world. She belonged to the London streets. Nib folks like the Bells weren't safe with her around.

Rachel was annoying, Molly thought. Always tagging along, hanging on to Molly's skirts with a sticky hand, demanding to be picked up or played with. But Rachel genuinely liked Molly, which nobody else did. And where had it gotten Rachel? Almost drowned, that's where. She would probably forgive Molly, because she was too young to know any better. But the rest of the family wouldn't. They would hate her forever.

Molly's eyes got blurry and she tripped on a tree root. For some stupid reason she was crying. It wasn't as if there was anything worth crying about. It was just too late for her to grow up decent like Captain Mattock had told her to, that was all. She'd done too much growing up indecent already.

The best thing she could do now was to get away from the Bells before she caused them any more trouble. They would be glad. They might be sad that they couldn't make her work anymore, but they could always buy another convict if they wanted.

She stopped walking. She was in a forest, among twisted, corkscrewed pine trees. She had never seen so many pine trees before. They were all around her, towering above her, and she couldn't see anything else. The sharp smell of pine sap filled the air, and the pine needles rustled and swished as they brushed against each other.

It was terrifying.

The forest seemed to be hovering over her, watching her. As if it were a person, or some sort of malevolent force. No: it was itself, and it didn't like intruders. It especially didn't like Molly, a child of the world's largest city, whose feet had always walked on paving stones and bricks.

That was ridiculous, Molly told herself. It was only a forest, a plaguey lot of trees. It didn't like or dislike anything. And it was a perfectly good place to hide while she figured out what to do next.

She took a deep breath and stepped off the path and into the woods. She made her way through poking branches that clung stickily to her hair, toward a place where she saw some light coming through the trees. She found a small clearing, just a few yards wide. There was high grass growing in it, and yellow flowers, the kind the New Yorkers called dent-de-lions and the Londoners called piss-in-beds. Beyond it was more forest. Molly wondered if the mass of looming, clutching trees extended all the way to Boston.

She had to go somewhere, and Boston was the only town she'd heard of up this way. Arabella's friend Christy had once mentioned that Boston was two weeks' journey away. By horse. And that was if you knew the way, because the trail was pretty hard to find in places, according to Christy. In between would be these lurking, hanging woods, and wild animals, and who knew what else. Out here, it wasn't so hard to believe there might be Salvages.

But Molly felt much safer in this patch of warm sunshine. She lay down in the grass and looked up at the pale blue summer sky. She needed to think what to do now. She needed to make a plan.

Instead, she fell asleep.

When she woke up, it was cold. The sun was no longer shining in the sky, and the birds were putting themselves to bed with a great deal of chatter and calling. Molly felt frightened again. She was more completely alone than she'd ever been in her life, and she didn't like it. She was also hungry. She was ashamed of this, because she realized she'd gotten so soft that she couldn't even go a whole day without eating. That's what living with nib folks had done to her.

117

There was a rustling in the trees. An animal. Maybe a bear. Molly scrambled to her feet and looked around, wondering if it was a good idea to run away. You weren't supposed to run from dogs; that just made them chase you. What about bears?

"Molly!" It was David's voice.

This was worse than a bear. Had he seen her yet? She moved into the cover of the trees, carefully. She ducked behind a pine and stood pressed against the trunk, on the shadowy side. A stick snapped under her foot.

Footsteps thumped on the dry pine needles. David came crashing through the hanging branches, out of breath. He saw her right away. "Molly! Why didn't you answer me?"

Molly backed away, looking around for a weapon. For two months she'd managed to avoid David, but now she'd run off and he'd found her alone. There was a jagged piece of broken branch by her foot, three feet long and as thick as her arm. She snatched it up and brandished it menacingly.

"You leave me be," she said.

"Molly, stop." He raised his hands, palms outward, in a conciliatory gesture. "Put that down."

"I'll put it down when you go away. Take one step closer and I'll smash your bleedin' mazzard." She put plenty of menace into her voice to make up for the fact that she barely came up to his chin.

David put his hands down and took a step backward. "My what?"

"Your mazzard. Head. I'll smash your bleedin' head. I mean it." She gestured with the sharp end of the branch. "I'll stow your glim."

David seemed to believe her, and to find the suggestion disturbing. He looked back over his shoulder, rather nervously, as if he too had just noticed that they were completely alone. Then he took a deep breath and calm seemed to settle over him, as it had that day in the kitchen when she grabbed the knife.

"Molly, put that down and come back with me. Everyone's half mad with worry."

"Then they can stop worrying, because I ain't coming back."

"Molly, you have to come back. You . . ." He trailed off as he searched for words. "You belong to us, you know. And everyone's all over town searching, and Father's notified the city watch."

"I ain't scared of no bleedin' constables," said Molly. "I bit the one that nabbed me in London." She took a step forward, waving the branch, and to her satisfaction David took a step backward. She advanced again, and David backed up again and then climbed up on a branch of a nearby pine tree. He stood on the branch and climbed up to a higher one. He did this with the unhurried air of having meant to do it all along.

"The watchmen aren't going to nab you. They're just looking for you because you're lost," he said from several feet over her head.

"I'm not lost. I'm buying a brush."

David chuckled. "There are no markets out here." He climbed higher.

" 'Buying a brush' means 'loping,' " said Molly irritably. "Running off." You weren't supposed to teach anybody Flash. If they didn't already know it, they weren't meant to know it. The trouble was, she was much better at speaking Flash than at the nib lingo David spoke. She looked up to try to see where David was. A few pine needles fell on her face. She could just make out the soles of his boots high above.

"But why are you running off? Don't you like living with us?"

"I don't live with you," said Molly. "I belong to you. You just said it."

David made an annoyed huffing noise. "Everyone belongs to someone."

"Not me."

"Molly, belonging to people is just . . . just the way things are." There was a scrambling sound, and bits of sticky pine-scented bark fell on Molly's upturned face. She couldn't see his boots anymore. "Even in London you must have belonged to people."

"I lived with them," Molly said. "And we kept out of each other's way. And one of them sang out beef on me, I think. Turned me in to the constables," she translated. "You don't do that to people who belong to you."

"Exactly," said David rather smugly, as if he'd just won the argument, even though he was the one hiding up in a tree.

Molly rested her weapon on the pine-needled ground and tried to see where David was. "What are you doing?"

"Looking at the trees. The tops of the trees." There was silence for a few minutes; then she saw him start to climb down. She didn't bother to raise her stick again. She was getting a lot less afraid of him now that she had chased him up a tree.

He sat on a branch just above her head and picked at a bit of pine resin on his hand. Molly could see the tiny wooden pegs that held together the leather soles of his boots. "Do you know what's out there?" he said, pointing into the woods.

"Boston," said Molly, feeling glum again. She could never survive that long journey in this grim, hostile forest. What would she eat? How would she keep things from eating her? And how would she ever get from Boston to London?

"No, Boston's that way." He waved dismissively to his right, then pointed again. "Over there is the North River. Some people call it Hudson's River. Father and I have sailed up it on a ship. There's a big trading post up north called Albany. Indians, and Dutchmen, and French. Fur traders, mostly."

Molly nodded, not taking her eyes off him. He could be trying to distract her so he could jump on her and grab the stick. But he didn't seem like a downy enough cove for that sort of dodge. Not by a long shot.

"The river goes between green mountains, and there are eagles circling overhead. Once Father and I climbed up a mountain; we climbed right up to the peak."

"Why?"

"To see." He smiled. "Well, Father thought it was rather mad too. And we saw what was beyond the mountains."

"What?"

"A sea of forest. As far as we could see into the distance, nothing but the tops of trees."

His face was glowing, as if he'd just described something marvelous. Molly just barely managed not to shrug.

"It felt as if the green and you were all part of the same single, living thing, as if you could jump from the mountaintop and soar over the forest, like an eagle, and you and the green would go on forever." He spread his arms as he said this, then nearly lost his balance and grabbed the tree trunk. He laughed. "Well. Father didn't feel that way about it, and I don't guess you do either."

Molly shook her head. She liked the idea of soaring. But wilderness frightened her, as it did any normal person.

"I'd like to be a voyageur," David went on. "You paddle a canoe into the wilderness, into places where hardly a human foot has stepped since the world was made. And you see the wild animals, moose and bears, and you talk the Indians' languages, and you trade with them for furs. You come back to the white men's country maybe once every couple of years or so."

"I thought you were going to run the warehouse with your father," Molly said tentatively. She didn't know why David was telling her all these strange ideas of his. She had enough problems of her own.

"Oh, I am." David smiled sadly. "It's no life for a good Jew, you know, being a voyageur. You can't keep the mitzvoth properly, or get ten men for a minyan. And you have to hunt animals; a Jew isn't supposed to do that." He sighed. "And Father would flip his wig if I even suggested it, and rend his garment, and that would just be to start with. Shall we go back now?"

Molly sighed too. "They're going to beat me."

"Well, probably. They were too worried not to." David looked at the darkening sky. "Too bad the Sabbath is over, or they couldn't. But don't tell me you're afraid of that. Or of anything, for that matter!" He laughed.

Molly was surprised at this description of herself. It seemed to her that she had been afraid all her life. "I made such a mess of things today," she said, surprising herself. "I make a mess of everything all the time."

"Who doesn't?" David swung down from the tree, landing beside Molly with a thump. His feet slipped on the pine needles, and he fell onto his back.

Molly tried not to smile, but David laughed, and so she couldn't help it.

"Let's go," said David. "Mother's out of her head, and everyone's running all over the island and praying for you."

Molly felt surprised again, because that made her sound as important as Rachel. "I bet Adah Grip isn't. I bet she's happy I'm gone."

"Well, sure," said David. "That proves it, doesn't it? If the Grip is happy, you can be pretty sure everyone else is miserable." He picked up the broken branch she had dropped. "This will be good for firewood. Let's go."

"They'll be talking about this Sabbath for a long

time," said David as they walked. "Running all over looking for Rachel, and then for you. And your Mrs. Wilkes charging right onto the main floor of the synagogue, bellowing—I thought old Mr. Frank would have an apoplexy."

Molly realized she had forgotten to tell Mrs. Wilkes that there was a separate door for women.

"How come your father patters Flash?" she asked.

"He what?"

"Speaks Flash-cant. Only cloves patter the lingo. Was he ever on the canting lay?"

"Say it in English," David suggested.

"A thief. Was he ever a thief?"

David laughed. "I don't think so. But I bet he's kept company with thieves. Father's been everywhere, and done everything." His voice suddenly became bitter. "When he was my age, he was traveling around the West Indies for his uncle's import business. Alone. And I'm not even allowed to go to Boston by myself, because I haven't had the smallpox. He went to Jamaica, Barbados—everywhere."

"Is that how he met your mother?" Molly asked.

"Uh-huh. They met at her father's molasses warehouse in Barbados. Then he went back to London and told his uncle, and"—David pantomimed writing a letter—"it was arranged."

This sounded considerably more complicated than how a mort and a cove got together in Seven Dials, but Molly suddenly felt that saying so would be embarrassing.

"I'll never get to travel like that if Father gets his way," David went on, swinging the branch lightly as they walked. "He won't even let me buy the smallpox."

"What's buying the smallpox?" said Molly.

"That's when they scratch you with some blood from a smallpox scab and you get sick for about two weeks; then you either get better or you die."

Molly cringed inwardly. "Why would you want to do that?"

"They say it's not as bad as smallpox that you catch. Most of the people that do it don't die," David said lightly.

"Yuck." Molly shook her head. "I don't know why people don't just go milk cows instead."

David looked at her oddly. "Milk cows?"

"Milkmaids never get smallpox. I heard that from some country morts that had come to . . . to work in London. Everybody in London knows that."

"Sounds like an old wives' tale to me." David frowned. "Why do you want to go back to London so much?"

"Who said I did?"

"I can tell from your voice. You say 'London' like it was, I don't know, the Promised Land."

"I don't say it like that! Don't make fun of my voice." Molly scowled.

"Well, sorry, but you do. But from what Father says, you were . . ." David seemed to change his mind about what he was going to say. "Things are pretty tough over there. So why would you want to go back? Do you have family?"

Molly felt tears well in her eyes, and she turned her head away angrily. "No," she said.

"Then why?"

She wasn't very good at answering questions like this. Because, she thought, my whole life hurts. I feel broken into a million pieces, and I just want to find whatever pieces I can.

"Because London is where I was born," she said. New York was just . . . a place far from London. A nowhere place. An edge place. A place on the edge of real.

He was still looking at her thoughtfully, so she added, "It's where I belong."

David shrugged. "If you say so. I don't see why you can't belong here."

Molly scowled and said nothing. He didn't know how it felt to be taken thousands of miles away from everything you ever knew. He didn't understand.

Nine

Mrs. Wilkes had been bought by a farmer in the village of Harlem, way up in the northern part of Manhattan island. That was why Molly hadn't seen her
before. She came to town only now and then, to help the
farmer's wife sell milk and eggs and cheeses at the market. A week after Mrs. Wilkes had helped to find Rachel,
Mrs. Bell sent Arabella and Molly to Harlem to buy
some eggs and to offer Mrs. Wilkes a shilling in thanks
for her help.

"But mind, be tactful about it," Mrs. Bell instructed
them. "If it seems as though it might embarrass her or
offend her to be offered the money, then don't offer it by
any means, but tell her how grateful we are and then just
buy the eggs. A dozen eggs."

Molly smiled to herself at the idea of Mrs. Wilkes
refusing the shilling. And Mrs. Wilkes didn't, of course.
She snapped it up and tucked it away in her apron. She

sold them the eggs, and gave them a squash and some dirty, lumpish things that she said were called potatoes. Arabella tied the eggs carefully in a handkerchief and put everything into her basket.

"I'm glad we found the poor chickabiddy, love," said Mrs. Wilkes. "I hate to see 'em drown. One of mine was drowned, you know, at Hungerford Stairs, while I was busy at Hungerford Market. And didn't hardly any of 'em live to get big. My, you've grown a sight yourself since leaving London."

Molly didn't see how she could have in only two months. She looked down at some chicken feathers stuck to the muddy ground of the dooryard.

Mrs. Wilkes looked from Molly to Arabella. "Those Bells must be treating you both right. Do they need any more serving wenches down there?"

"I don't believe so," said Arabella. Her eyes were narrowed in an expression Molly took for disapproval. It was the same expression Arabella often had when she looked at Molly.

"Pity. My people here aren't bad, you know. When they're sober. They do have plenty to eat in this here New York colony, don't they? Even if there's not much rhino."

"Rhino?" said Arabella.

"Redge," said Mrs. Wilkes. "Ginglers."

Arabella looked at Mrs. Wilkes as if she had lost her mind.

"Money," Molly translated.

"Exactly," said Mrs. Wilkes. "Have you noticed it, dears? They use food for money. Or they write it all down in a book. Or they use this stuff." She reached into her apron and drew out a long string of purple-and-white shell beads.

"Seawant," said Arabella. "We've always used that for money in New York. But it doesn't buy as much as it used to." She looked toward the lane and nudged Molly.

"Well, I've heard it called wampum too," said Mrs. Wilkes. "But call it what you will, it ain't coin of the realm. This here is the first honest grunter I've touched since I left London." She caressed the shilling in her pocket. "Which I much want to talk to you about, child." She turned to Molly. "Being down there in town as you are, it's easier for you to . . ."

A woman's voice inside the farmhouse called "Lizzie! Get your sorry bumpkin in here and murther these chickens!"

"It's time we were going," said Arabella firmly.

Molly and Arabella went back along the footpath called the Bowery. As soon as they lost sight of the farm, Arabella reached into the basket and took out the potatoes. They looked like rocks covered in dirt.

"Filthy things," she said, flinging them into the tall grass.

"Hey!" Molly ran into the brush and got down on

her knees, parting the weeds as she searched for the potatoes. "That's scran. You don't throw scran away."

"Not if 'scran' means 'food,' it's not," said Arabella, watching her. "Nobody's going to eat anything that looks like that."

"We are." Molly finally found the last potato and tied all of them up in her apron. She didn't trust Arabella not to throw them away again. Molly had never thrown away anything that could be eaten.

They walked on in silence for an hour or so, following the Bowery through small patches of woods, in and out of sight of the river. Molly listened to the crickets and frogs chirping in the tall grass, and the trickle of water from the streams and rills they passed over.

After a while, Arabella took a deep breath and said, "Molly, I don't know what it's like over there in London."

Molly waited to see what else Arabella would say.

"But some of those people that come over here from over there are folks that I don't think a girl ought to know."

"Mrs. Wilkes cuts bene. She's been kind to me," Molly said defensively.

"Yes, I can see that she's a kind woman," said Arabella. "But kind people, you see, Molly, aren't always . . ." She seemed to turn her words over in her head for a minute. "Don't always do what's right," she finished.

Molly could have told Arabella that herself. Doing what was right wasn't something you could afford to think about in London. You thought about staying alive: who could help you do it, and who could stop you from doing it. People like Mrs. Wilkes had helped Molly stay alive ever since . . . well, for years. They weren't terribly reliable, of course. You let them help you when they were willing to. But you didn't rely on anybody except yourself.

Molly and Arabella walked for another hour or so in silence. Molly thought about what Mrs. Wilkes had said. It was true; there didn't seem to be very much real money in America. She remembered how Mr. Bell had bought her, half with money and half with things from his shop. And she had heard someone say that the land for the synagogue had cost the congregation a hundred pounds sterling, a loaf of sugar, and a pound of tea— although, Molly thought, you could also say that somebody had bought the hundred pounds, the pound of tea, and the loaf of sugar for the land that the synagogue was built on. It worked both ways.

It made Molly feel clever to have thought of that. It was the sort of thing that Mr. Bell and David and the other men would say in their arguments.

"There were three babies that died in between David and Rachel," said Arabella unexpectedly. Molly had forgotten she was there and looked at her, startled. Arabella counted off on her fingers. "Micha, and Adah, and another one also called Rachel. That's why Mrs. Bell worries a bit."

Molly nodded. That was normal. In London, most babies died. Molly thought of the distant look Mrs. Bell so often had. Maybe she wasn't seeing Barbados when she looked like that. Maybe she was seeing the three babies who had died. She wondered why Arabella was telling her this.

Arabella had become silent again, and Molly went back to thinking about what Mrs. Wilkes had started to talk about. Stealing. The lack of real money was what made it difficult for a pickpocket to make any sort of honest living in New York. You couldn't filch a barrel of wheat from a cash drawer when no one was looking, or hide a gallon of rum in your sleeves.

Mrs. Wilkes must have gotten back into the canting lay, back into picking up a few odds and ends and selling them. Molly had seen her trying to pick that flat's pocket in the market. Mrs. Wilkes probably wanted Molly as a partner. Maybe together they could find a fencing cull to buy whatever they might be able to find lying around. Or maybe Mrs. Wilkes had already found one.

Well, Arabella was right. That sort of trouble, Molly didn't need. She thought about Moses What's-his-face, the cove who was hanged for stealing in New York after he'd been transported for stealing in London.

She thought about the whipping post at the end of Broad Street too. Getting tied to the post and whipped in front of a crowd of onlookers would be as bad as being hanged—worse, because you wouldn't be able to make a brave show of it.

But then, Molly thought, for only four pounds she could buy passage back to London. Now, that was something worth thinking about. Twenty shillings made a pound. Twenty times four was . . . was . . . Molly couldn't think how much twenty times four was. She started counting on her fingers, but silently, and with her hands tucked into her sleeves, because she didn't want Arabella to know what she was thinking.

The path widened into a road, and Molly felt the hard cobblestones through the soles of her moccasins again. It was sunset as they passed into the city—it had taken them all day to walk to Harlem and back. The lengthening shadows of trees and houses cooled the street, and Molly noticed one oddly shaped shadow, like an inverted L. She looked up and saw that it was the shadow of the gallows. The nubbing-cheat. A small one, built for just one customer at a time. Not like Tyburn Tree in London, which had room to turn off nine at one go.

At home, Mrs. Bell was slicing bread and kosher cheese for supper. Molly didn't look at her, because she wouldn't speak to Mrs. Bell since Mrs. Bell had whipped Molly for losing Rachel and for running off and getting lost herself. She hadn't really whipped her, but she'd pulled Molly out of the kitchen into the backyard while Mr. Bell and David averted their eyes politely. She'd grabbed a dry, rotten stick off the kindling pile and flailed at Molly, who turned and twisted in her grip and managed to avoid getting hit more than once or twice before the stick finally fell to pieces.

Although Molly wasn't speaking to Mrs. Bell, Mrs. Bell did not seem to have noticed. "Take this bread and cheese along to Mr. Bell and David, Molly, dear," she said, pushing a tied-up handkerchief across the table. "They're taking inventory, counting everything, and they'll be at it till late."

Molly grabbed the bundle without looking at Mrs. Bell and thrust it into her apron with the potatoes. She didn't want to leave the potatoes in the kitchen; Arabella or Mrs. Bell might throw them out. She started down to Dock Street. It was almost dark now, and the tree frogs had come out and were chirping all around. When Molly got to Bell's Chandlery and Ships' Furnishings, she stopped.

Through the window she could see René Duguay, the ship's captain she'd met when she lost Rachel. He was in his high-topped boots and sweeping ostrich-plumed hat, which he hadn't bothered to remove indoors. He was examining a length of rope that Mr. Bell was holding.

Molly went into the shop. With its wooden walls

and floor, it always felt oddly like being in a ship. The shop smelled faintly of rum (unless that was Captain Duguay) and of ship's biscuits, which brought back nauseating memories of the *Good Intention*. Mr. Bell was at the counter, running his finger down a list of numbers in a leather-bound book and explaining why the cost of rope had gone up. Molly set the bread and cheese down on the counter beside him.

Mr. Bell looked up. "Hello, Molly. Go take a look at what we turned up in our inventory," he said, nodding toward the door at the back of the shop that led to the warehouse.

David appeared at the door. "Molly! Come see what we found on the rope coils."

Molly noticed that David's smile was warm. She smiled back. How could she have thought he was dangerous?

The warehouse was dim, and full of the harsh smells of canvas and rope. Molly followed David back, through narrow passages between the high stacks of bales of canvas and barrels of meal, to the coils of rope. In the middle of a coil lay one of the warehouse cats, surrounded by a pile of tiny, hairless animals with their eyes shut.

Molly stopped in surprise. "Oh! What are they?"

David laughed. "What are they? Kittens, of course."

Now that Molly looked closely, she could see that they had tiny little cats' ears folded on their heads, and very thin fur with striped markings. She had never seen kittens so young before; that was all. Her face burned at having said something so stupid. "Can I pick one up?"

"Father says no. Not till they're a week old, because they're very delicate. But you can pet them, see, like this." David reached out one finger and gently stroked the back of one of the squirming creatures.

Molly knelt and touched one of the kittens. She ran her finger down its warm little back to its tiny scrap of tail. The tail curled around her finger. The mother cat watched Molly warily.

The door to the warehouse creaked. Mr. Bell and René Duguay had come in to look at the rope the captain wanted. Mr. Bell held a candle, which he shone on the rope and on Molly and David and the kittens.

"Kittens, eh?" said René Duguay. "Better drown 'em. I'll take the rope without the kittens."

"I'll give the kittens to my friends," said Mr. Bell calmly. "Everyone needs a few good cats. These coils of hawser-laid are ten ells long, and I have shroud-laid rope in the corner." Molly had noticed that much as Jewish men liked to argue with each other, they tried not to argue with men who weren't Jewish. As long as René Duguay didn't actually try to drown the kittens, there would be no fuss.

Molly felt as if René Duguay was looking at her, and not the ropes. The feeling made her very uncomfortable. She thought she had better go home. She no longer thought that she wanted to work her passage with him, even if it meant getting back to England.

She curtseyed as Mrs. Bell had taught her and made her way out through the dark warehouse and the shop.

She had hardly reached the cobbled street when René Duguay was beside her.

"Well met, miss," he said, as if he hadn't followed her. "Are you still looking for passage to England?"

"No," said Molly, turning quickly to walk away. "I've decided not to travel just now."

The captain put an arm around her shoulders. "Ah, that's because you haven't seen my ship yet. Come and have a look."

Molly tried to duck under his arm, but his hand gripped her shoulder tightly. She jammed her elbow into his belly as hard as she could. He let go of her with a startled yelp, and then reached for his belt. Molly saw the flash of a dagger there. She swung her apron full of potatoes and hit him in the arm.

"Master Duguay!" Mr. Bell and David were standing beside them. The captain straightened up hastily and adjusted his coat to hide the dagger.

"I'll have to . . ." Mr. Bell was furious, and Molly could tell he was trying hard to control himself. "I'll have to ask you not to interfere with the women in my family."

"I was just having a bit of fun with the serving

wench," said Captain Duguay easily. "She doesn't mind."

"I mind," said Mr. Bell. "My servants are family. And I must ask you not to pay your addresses to them."

Mr. Bell and Captain Duguay looked at each other for a moment. Neither spoke. Molly thought that Mr. Bell's look was hot and Captain Duguay's was cold. She watched their eyes do battle.

"Well!" said Captain Duguay with a shrug. "There are plenty of other merchants in this town I can buy from."

"Yes," said Mr. Bell. "There are."

Captain Duguay turned on his heel and walked away.

Molly watched him go. She knew he had just told Mr. Bell that he wasn't going to buy supplies from him anymore. Mr. Bell had just lost a lot of money from that argument. It was one more thing she had made a mess of.

"I'm sorry," she muttered.

"Well, I'm not!" said David angrily. "I'm glad he's taking his business elsewhere, the filthy old pirate."

"It wasn't your fault, Molly," said Mr. Bell wearily. "And, David, we have to do business with privateers. Privateers are half of what keeps New York alive, you know. Especially now that times are hard."

"They can call themselves privateers, but I call them pirates," said David.

Molly thought they were going to get into an argument about the difference between pirates and privateers, which was good because it would distract them. She was afraid that they might discover that she had spoken to Captain Duguay before, and then they might realize that she'd been asking about passage to London.

But Mr. Bell just sighed and said, "David, walk Molly home, lad. These New York streets aren't as safe as they used to be."

Ten

Molly knew there was no point in talking to another ship's captain until she could get together four pounds for her passage. She was in the Bells' yard thinking about how to do this when Mrs. Wilkes stopped by. Mrs. Wilkes had indeed found a fencing cull.

"Coo, love. Are you alone?" Mrs. Wilkes hissed.

"There's morts in the kitchen." Molly nodded over her shoulder. Arabella was inside with Christy and Rose, another friend she went to church with. Mrs. Bell had gone to the Myerses' yard to boil a great kettle of kosher soap with some other women. She'd taken Rachel with her.

Mrs. Wilkes looked around hastily, then squatted down and began helping Molly pick stones out of a heap of dried peas. "Do you know John Hughson, who owns the Fool's Tavern?"

"No," said Molly. She knew where the tavern was;

she had seen its painted sign, with a picture of a jester in a belled hat holding a bag of coins, and the words "A Fool and His Money," which Molly had just recently realized with pride that she could read. Next to the sign was a bush, the traditional symbol of a tavern, nailed to the wall for the benefit of those who couldn't read.

Mrs. Wilkes picked up a dried pea and popped it into her mouth, chewing thoughtfully. "Well, it's a wild enough place, and I don't suppose your folks would let you go near it. But it's a stalling-ken; the Hughson cove and his mort are fencing culls. And you get better value for your goods in New York than over in London town when they've got any blunt to pay you with."

Molly listened with interest. "Have you spoken with anything, then?" she asked. To "speak with" something was Flash for stealing it.

"Nay, let's not speak of what I've spoken with," said Mrs. Wilkes. "But I thought I'd tip you the wink, in case you didn't know. That's all."

"You can be done over for filching in New York," said Molly. "Haven't you seen the nubbing-cheat?" She thought of the inverted L standing out black against the sunset, and shuddered.

Mrs. Wilkes shrugged. "No different from London. And we're bound to come to it sooner or later, child. The important thing, when your time comes, is to make a brave show of it. It's what we're born for."

Molly picked idly at the peas and looked at Mrs.

Wilkes thoughtfully. She didn't know what she had been born for, but she was pretty sure it wasn't hanging. There had to be more to life than that. "Do you ever think about going back to London?" she asked.

Mrs. Wilkes shook her head firmly. "No, not till my seven years are up, and don't you either, ducks. There's no call to go looking for a case of hempen fever before your time."

"Then what do you want to steal for?" Molly asked, scooping up a handful of peas and letting them run through her fingers.

"Hsst, child! Watch your language!"

Molly corrected herself: "To file the cly, I mean."

"Because it's what we do, isn't it?" said Mrs. Wilkes. "For a living. A mort's got to do what she does for a living. I'd hate to get back to London in seven years' time and find these fambles had lost their touch at the figging lay." She flexed her fingers expertly.

Molly stared at her own hands. She knew they had gotten harder and more callused from hauling heavy buckets of water. Hot water and hot cooking fires, lye soap and salting meat from the shochet, and rough bark-covered logs had made her fingers less sensitive. She wriggled them experimentally and thought they seemed stiffer than they had once been.

But Mrs. Bell often praised her sewing, and told her she had nimble fingers. Nimble enough for sewing, maybe. But would she still be able to pick pockets?

"Anyway, the Hughson cove is the one," said Mrs. Wilkes. "And if you should happen to snaffle anything yourself and daren't go near the Fool's, why, I'll be in town every Saturday, and I can carry it for you."

Mrs. Wilkes wasn't offering a favor. She would take a cut of the price for herself, Molly knew—probably half. But it was true that the Bells wouldn't hear of Molly going into a tavern. And how else was she going to get four pounds? She needed to get it fast in order to get back to London before she'd lost her skill at the figging lay completely.

"Well, I'd best be going," said Mrs. Wilkes. "But let me know."

"All right," said Molly.

The thing was, Molly reflected as she stirred the peas with her hand and then spread them smooth again, that she still hadn't seen anything she could speak with. In the Bells' house, nothing was worth much: the dishes were of wood or clay; the pots were old; the spoons were made of horn or pewter. The Bells hardly ever seemed to have any actual money. The clothes and the books probably weren't worth snaffling—in a town as small as New York, a fencing cull wouldn't risk buying something that could be identified so easily. And everything in the Bells' warehouse was too big to steal.

And where else did she ever go? The market sold food, mostly, and there wasn't much cash used there. She thought about the man she'd seen having his tooth pulled. You probably couldn't even get away with an easy dodge like that—picking a flat's pocket while he was having his tooth pulled—at the market in New York. It was too small, and there was nowhere to hide. She thought again about Moses What's-his-face, who had been hanged for stealing gold. Where the blue blazes had he found any gold to steal? Not at the market, Molly was sure. And she hardly ever went anywhere else except to the synagogue. The synagogue was just a synagogue; there was really nothing in it but the ark, and the Torah scrolls, and . . .

Molly stopped and stared at the peas spread out in front of her.

And the silver breastplates and the rimonim, the silver crowns and bells and medallions that decorated the ends of the scrolls!

Molly gathered the peas up and poured them into a wooden bowl. She carried the bowl into the house, carefully composing her face as she'd learned to do when she was very small, so that none of her thoughts showed.

Arabella, Christy, and Rose were sitting on a settle near the fire, deep in conversation. They stopped talking as soon as Molly came in. Then Arabella started talking, loudly, about how hard it had rained the night before. The other women agreed that it had rained very hard. Molly didn't pay much attention to them, although she noticed that Christy had a deep scratch on her face. Molly was busy thinking about the silver on the Torah scrolls. Was she sure it was silver? Yes, of course. She knew the white glint of silver very well, even at a distance.

There was a kettle of water already boiling on the hod in the fireplace, and Molly poured the peas into it, holding her skirts back carefully from the flames as she did so. She thought of the pease porridge Mr. Mendez had paid for her to eat every day at Newgate. On Sundays there used to be a small lump of ham floating in the porridge as a special treat. Molly's stomach did a flip-flop as she thought of the ham. She'd gotten used to thinking about the Jewish dietary laws when she cooked, and taking care not to break them. Ham wasn't kosher; ham was terayfa. Well, when she got back to London, maybe she wouldn't eat ham. At least not if there was anything else to eat.

The trouble was, there often wasn't all that much to eat in London. Molly remembered the times when she and Mama would carefully split the last bit of a penny loaf between them, gnawing on it slowly to make it seem like more.

Mama had always been kind about sharing things. Once, when Molly's dress had fallen apart, Mama had gone out and sold her own cloak to buy a secondhand dress for Molly from a ragman.

With a start, Molly looked down at the dress she was wearing. The scowring-cheats she had now were too clean, too good. She wouldn't last a day in Seven

Dials in Mrs. Bell's hand-me-down dress and petticoats. She ran a hand thoughtfully over the warm, tightly woven woolen broadcloth. Then she pulled up her skirts and looked at her ragged, much-darned stockings. They, at least, were hers. The stockings were a part of who she really was, and they would fit in in Seven Dials. But when she got to London, she'd have to sell her dress and petticoats, Molly thought sadly.

She remembered how she and Mama used to laugh at morts dressed the way Molly was dressed now. If Mama could see her now, Mama wouldn't know her. Or would think she'd turned into a bleedin' nib mort like the highfalutin serving maids the two of them used to throw horse dung at if they wandered into Seven Dials by mistake.

A shout interrupted Molly's thoughts. The African women had gone out into the yard and were arguing. It sounded like Arabella and Rose were scolding the younger woman, Christy. But Christy was talking back. Their voices rose in discord. Molly stepped to the door and looked out into the yard. She saw Arabella and Rose standing side by side, both looking angry. Arabella was holding Christy by the arm and giving her a shake to emphasize what she was saying. Christy was glaring back, defiant. Molly heard Christy say what sounded like "But I wasn't even born yet in 1712!" Then Christy saw Molly. All three women looked at her. Then they turned quickly and strolled out of the yard.

Molly turned and went back to the fireplace to stir the pease porridge. Let them have their secrets, she thought. They didn't trust her any more than anyone else did. She needed to get back home to London, where she belonged. Where everyone didn't look at her as if she were some kind of mistake.

She went to the salt box, took out a pinch of salt, dropped it into the pease porridge, and gave the pot another stir with the long wooden spoon. The Torah scrolls were kept at the east end of the synagogue, on the main floor, where she had never set foot. Both doors to the synagogue—the main door that the men used and the side door to the women's balcony—were locked. In London, Molly had been learning to pick locks with a pair of lockpicks that she'd inherited from a dubber who had ridden the three-legged mare at Tyburn. But she'd had to throw the lockpicks away when she was taken by the constables.

There were other ways to deal with locks, of course. Molly would have to take a closer look. Then she'd know what to do.

Eleven

As summer gave way to fall, the warehouse kittens grew into stiff-legged, furry little adventurers. Their eyes had opened wide and blue, and their tails stuck straight up in the air as they stumbled about in the piles of rope, falling to the floor and mewling hysterically as they clawed their way back up. They were in the way at the warehouse, so Mr. Bell and David brought the kittens and their mother to the house, where they were also in the way, scrabbling around the brick floor of the kitchen and pouncing on the women's skirts as they brushed by.

In the evenings, when Rachel had been put, protesting, to bed and the family was gathered around the parlor fire to read and study, the mother cat would settle down by the fireplace and call the kittens to nurse with a single sharp meow. Then the cat family would fall asleep beside the fire while the human family studied.

Molly had finished *The English Spelling Book* and was reading a book called *The English Schoolmaster and Child's Moral Companion*. She was still having trouble with the alphabet, though. Especially with the *s*'s, that looked like *f*'s.

She turned a page and read aloud to Arabella, " 'Young boy, you muft learn to be wife.' "

Everyone laughed. Molly started to scowl, and then found herself laughing too. Well, it was a stupid thing for a book to say, anyway.

"Never mind, love," said Mrs. Bell. "You're doing fine. You'll be teaching little Rachel her letters before we know it."

Molly thought that if she could get the silver from the scrolls in the synagogue, she'd be gone long before Rachel was ready to learn her letters. For some reason, the thought didn't make her as happy as it should have.

" 'Must,' " said Arabella. "See? 'Wise.' Read it again."

Mr. Bell was poring over a letter from London, occasionally reading bits of it to the rest of the family. The letter wasn't addressed to him, but was full of messages from Jews in London, and had been handed around from one Jewish family to another in New York.

"It seems we're planning to join Mr. Oglethorpe's new colony, called Georgia," he said.

"Really?" Mrs. Bell looked up from one of Rachel's smocks that she was mending. "They're letting us in?"

Molly could tell from their tone of voice that in this

conversation, "us" and "we" meant Jews. The Bells themselves weren't joining any new colony.

"Only by accident," said Mr. Bell. "But that's good enough for us. Listen to what Mr. Oglethorpe said. He said that the new colony would be open to settlers of 'all Persuasions in Religion, except Papists.' "

Mrs. Bell and David both laughed. "And we're not Papists, are we?" David said. "Father, can we . . ."

"No," said Mr. Bell, frowning. This time Molly knew that David had used "we" to mean the Bells. Or at least the male Bells.

"Well, then, couldn't I . . ."

"No," Mr. Bell repeated. "We don't know how safe it is, or how those other settlers will react when they find themselves surrounded by Jews. And besides, you've never had the smallpox."

David said nothing, but looked mutinous.

"There's a message here from Israel Mendez for you, Molly," said Mr. Bell, clearly wanting to change the subject. "He sends his best wishes."

"Can I read it?" said Molly, putting down the *Child's Moral Companion.*

Mr. Bell looked uncomfortable. "Um, it's a bit . . . Well, Mendez is an unusual fellow."

By this time, everyone was looking at Mr. Bell, who seemed to wish he hadn't brought up the matter. "The handwriting's terrible," he said.

Molly stood up and went over to look at the letter.

"He's a sanctimonious, mealymouthed, self-satisfied idiot!" said Mr. Bell, throwing the letter into the fire. Molly started, as she always did when Mr. Bell lost his temper like that, but nobody else seemed very impressed.

"Now, Ephraim," said Mrs. Bell calmly. She put down Rachel's smock and deftly plucked the letter from the fire. "The Franks haven't read this yet," she said, beating out the flames at the edge with her palm. She scanned the letter. "Oh! That wretched—"

Molly grabbed the letter out of her hand and dodged behind the table, out of reach. It was a big sheet of foolscap, both sides crammed with writing. The paper was worn from much folding and unfolding, and now charred along one edge as well. Molly scanned it until she found her own name, Mary Abraham. Since she could only read aloud, she did.

"'I am pleafed to learn that Mary Abraham ar-arrived, and has been taken in by the Bells. Give her my regrets—no, regards—and tell her I hope that, re-moved from the foul fink—sink—of her evil ways, she has—seized?—to be a blot and ftain on the cloak of our poo—no, our people, Ifrael.'" She put the letter down on the table.

"Oh, I could slap that man!" said Mrs. Bell. "He knew everyone would read it!"

Molly shrugged. What the letter said about her wasn't very nice, but she'd been called worse things. "Mr.

Mendez paid for me when I was in N—before I came here," she said fairly. "He paid for my food and my—" She looked at David and decided not to say "chains" or "cell." Of course David and everybody else knew she'd been in Newgate, but she didn't feel like talking about it when they were all looking at her. "My keep."

"Yes, he's a very charitable man," said Mrs. Bell, in the same tone she might have used to say "he eats kittens." Molly realized that the Bells knew Mr. Mendez— Mr. Mendez, whom her mother had once chased with a knife. Suddenly it seemed as if the ocean that had taken two months to cross, that had nearly swallowed the *Good Intention*, was no wider than the distance from the Bells' house to the synagogue.

"Do you know Mr. Lopez too?" she said. "He brought me an orange."

"He would," said Mr. Bell. "Good old Lopez."

"Israel Mendez always did think that charity just meant spending money," said Mrs. Bell, folding her arms.

Had the Bells known her mother? Molly thought. Surely they would have said so before. Her mother never went near the synagogue, never had anything to do with other Jews. Molly wondered why. Her mother had never said. It seemed to Molly now as if there were things her mother had built a wall around, things that Molly somehow knew she was never allowed to mention.

A crash at the kitchen door made them all jump.

Molly seized the iron poker from beside the fireplace. A girl's voice screamed "Arabella! Arabella!"

Everyone else was in the kitchen in an instant. Molly followed behind, clutching the poker. Mrs. Bell unlocked the door with the great iron key and a figure stumbled out of the night and collapsed into her arms.

"Christy," Arabella breathed.

"Blankets, Molly!" Mrs. Bell snapped.

Molly dropped the poker and ran to drag the blankets off the cabinet bed, grateful for an excuse not to look at Christy. The hot, sickly smell of blood and fear took her back in an instant to London, to a night at the Bleeding Hart in Dogwell Lane when Sim Dimber got bowzy on blue gin and started laying about him with a shovel, holding the whole room hostage to his rage until he finally decided whom to kill.

"Molly!" Mrs. Bell snapped.

Molly hurriedly dumped the blankets onto the floor in a heap. Then Arabella and Mrs. Bell lifted Christy gently onto one of the blankets.

Christy was alive but only just. Her skin was covered with welts crisscrossed on top of welts and blood running out of the gashes on top. Molly had seen people whipped in London, of course, but not on their faces like this.

Christy's breath rattled in and out of her mouth, forming small bubbles of blood on her lips. She seemed to be unconscious. Molly hoped so.

"Molly! Look alive. Get warm water, and some rags," said Mrs. Bell sharply.

Molly stood up shakily and stumbled to the fireplace. She swung the crane away from the fire, braced her foot against the raised hearth, and heaved at the wire handle of the kettle. Then Arabella was beside her, lifting the kettle off the crane and calling out "Rags, Molly!" in the middle of a Christian prayer that she was muttering rapidly. Molly ran into the pantry for the ragbag. She brought it out and dumped its contents beside Mrs. Bell, accidentally catching sight of Christy again.

The puffs and gashes on Christy's face had closed both her eyes and obscured her features. The red streaks of blood seemed to stand out even more strongly than they were before.

"She's losing color," said Arabella. "Look at her lips." Molly couldn't even tell where the lips began on Christy's disfigured face.

"Then we may lose her," said Mrs. Bell, almost to herself. "Where's that boy with the brandy?"

Molly noticed for the first time that David and Mr. Bell were gone. Just then David burst through the back door with a brandy flask. Arabella grabbed it out of his hand, pulling out the cork while Mrs. Bell lifted Christy's head and shoulders. They managed to force a little brandy down Christy's throat. Within a moment, the horrible gray color had left her lips. Her eyes were half open but were focused on nothing.

Mr. Bell came running in with Dr. Alvarez, one of the men who sometimes came to the Bells' house in the evenings to read in Hebrew and argue. His wig was off, and the fashionable pink turban he was wearing instead had slid down his bald head and hung over one ear at an odd angle. Dr. Alvarez dropped to his knees beside Christy. He took her wrist in his hand and counted her pulse against his pocket watch. It was a silver pocket watch, Molly noticed, on a silver chain with some fobs that looked like gold.

"The pulse is very weak," he said. "Take those blankets and cover her up."

"But the wounds . . . ," said Mrs. Bell.

"First things first," said Dr. Alvarez. "The spirit must be kept in the body. Then we'll worry about the wounds."

They took the blankets Molly had dropped on the floor and covered Christy up to her chin. Dr. Alvarez kept a hand on her wrist and kept checking her pulse against his watch—a solid silver scout that would have brought one pound twelve in London, not counting the chain and fobs, Molly thought. But just now she wasn't even that interested in it.

"What happened here?" asked Dr. Alvarez.

"She just arrived at our kitchen door like this," said

Mr. Bell. "A short time ago. Obviously she's been whipped."

"In a most abominable fashion," Dr. Alvarez remarked. "By whom?"

Mr. Bell shook his head. "I don't even know the wench, to tell the truth," he said.

Dr. Alvarez looked at Arabella.

"Her name's Christy. She belongs to Mr. Grant, the cordwainer," said Arabella tensely. "He often beats her for no reason. He takes against her because her father was one of them burned in 1712."

At the mention of 1712, everyone nodded. Molly wondered what 1712 had to do with anything.

"Christy never does anything to displease him," said Arabella, her voice tight with suppressed anger. "But Mr. Grant thinks she's bound to turn out a rebel and burn down white people's houses. He says blood will tell."

"Hmm." Dr. Alvarez frowned. "I place no credit in such beliefs myself."

"Nor do I, usually," said Mr. Bell, "though one sees signs of it at times." Molly found the men's calm infuriating. She wanted Mr. Bell to lose his temper and go beat Mr. Grant, whoever he was. Dr. Alvarez kept attending to Christy.

"The pulse improves," he said. "Has anyone complained to the magistrates about this Mr. Grant?"

Arabella shook her head impatiently. "What good would that do? He owns her."

"Nonetheless, there are limits to what's allowed," said Mr. Bell.

"Yes," said Dr. Alvarez. "And certainly this beating, deserved or not, exceeds those limits, since we fear for the patient's life."

"It doesn't matter," said Arabella through clenched teeth.

"Matter? Of course it matters!" said Dr. Alvarez. "The girl is half dead! I know that negroes aren't allowed to testify against white men in court, but I can certainly give evidence that the patient was sadly abused."

"And so can I," said Mr. Bell.

"It doesn't matter." Arabella got up from her knees and stood looking up at Mr. Bell. "It doesn't matter. Don't you understand? He owns her. Even if you testify, even if he's found guilty in the court, he still owns her." She was trembling now, her fists clenched at her sides.

"That doesn't give him the right to try to kill her. And the court can order him to sell her if it's determined that he makes a habit of maltreating her," said Mr. Bell reasonably.

Mrs. Bell rose and put a calming hand on Arabella's shoulder. Arabella shook it off angrily. "It doesn't matter what the law says!" she cried. "And it doesn't matter what the magistrates say, or what you testify to them, or what your doctor friend testifies to them! None of your fool laws is going to keep Christy alive if Mr. Grant has it in his mind to kill her. Because the court only meets now and then, and he owns her every blessed moment of her whole blessed life." She took a deep breath and let it out slowly. "Until the grave sets her free."

Everyone looked at Arabella in surprise. Molly was impressed. She didn't think she'd have had the nerve to yell at Mr. Bell herself. Snap at him, maybe. Certainly nothing more than that.

Dr. Alvarez stared at Arabella and shook his head. He turned back to Christy. "The pulse is stable enough," he said. "But I don't care for this blood issuing from the mouth." He pried Christy's mouth open gently and peered inside. "Bring me a candle," he said. Since Mrs. Bell was busy mixing up a hot posset of milk and ale, Molly got a candlestick from the table. She lit it by sticking it into the kitchen fire, in the way that Mrs. Bell always told her not to.

"There are cuts inside the mouth. Let's hope that's all it is," said Dr. Alvarez, poking around in Christy's mouth with his finger. Christy's eyes stayed unfocused, Molly noticed, as she held the candle for him. Molly's hand shook, and she splashed hot beeswax on Dr. Alvarez's hand. He yelped.

"Sorry," Molly said, putting the candle down in its tin holder.

Dr. Alvarez irritably picked blobs of wax off his hand. "I'm afraid it's entirely necessary that we make a magistrate's case of this," he said to Arabella. "Your friend won't survive another such attack."

"Some things are too important to argue about," Arabella muttered, more to herself than to him.

Mr. Bell, Molly realized, had been staring at Arabella in silence for several minutes. Ever since she'd yelled at him.

It wasn't his hot, angry look. It was just a very surprised look.

"Who is going to sit up with the patient?" asked Dr. Alvarez.

"I will," said Arabella.

"Arabella and I will take turns," said Mrs. Bell. At Arabella's surprised look, she added, "It's a mitzvah. Molly, you'll sleep with Rachel tonight." She ladled hot posset into a tankard and handed it to Molly. "You take a good drink of that first. You're shaking like a leaf."

Molly took the tankard and sat down on the settle with relief, because her legs were trembling and were just about to give out. She gulped the warm milk and ale and felt calmer. She was ashamed of herself for being so easily rattled. It wasn't as if she hadn't seen worse things in her life than Christy's injuries. She just hadn't seen them in the Bells' warm kitchen.

She wasn't quite sure why that mattered, so she took another sip of posset.

"Why is it a mitzvah to sit up with Christy?" she whispered to David when he came and sat beside her on the settle.

"Taking care of the sick is a mitzvah," said David, reaching for her cup and taking a long drink. The Bells, like most people, didn't have enough cups and tankards to go around. "And so is visiting them. And you can never leave someone to die alone; that's one of the most important mitzvoth."

Suddenly Molly felt sick, as if all the cuts and welts on Christy's face were on her own insides. David tried to give the posset back to her, but she waved it aside.

"Don't worry. I don't think Christy's going to die," he whispered reassuringly. "Dr. Alvarez is a very good doctor, you know. And Christy's young and strong."

But that wasn't what was wrong. Molly felt herself growing cold. She didn't want to think about what was wrong. She wanted to run out of the room, away from what David had just said. She stood up slowly, her knees trembling. "I think I'll go to bed now," she said. She ran upstairs to Rachel and David's bedroom and climbed into bed beside Rachel. She lay awake for a long time, trembling and trying not to think. But David's words kept repeating in her head: you can never leave someone to die alone.

Twelve

If things like this could happen in New York—
things like what Mr. Grant had done to Christy—then
Molly definitely needed to get back to London as soon
as possible. In London, she had often seen people hurt
other people, but she had always managed to get away
alive. She remembered when Crabbed Ben had chived
his mort Nellie with a broken gin bottle in a garret in
Fryingpan Alley, where Molly was living with the both
of them and a few maunderers from Thieving Lane.
Molly had lit out for Seven Dials at once and never
come back. She'd never had to see any of those people
again, except at a distance. In New York, you couldn't
avoid people that way. There was nowhere to get away
to. There was nowhere to run.

So she kept studying the problem of getting to the
scrolls. There were two locks on the synagogue. The
lock on the women's door was a simple ward lock. Those

could easily be picked, Molly knew, with a makeshift key. But that door didn't lead to anything valuable. There was nothing in the women's balcony worth taking. And the wooden lattice, like a fence from the rail to the ceiling, divided it from the main floor of the synagogue below.

It was harder to tell about the lock on the main door. Molly doubted if it was a simple ward lock. Not with all that silver in the ark just waiting to be carried away. Molly managed to examine it late one night when Mrs. Bell and Arabella were busy with Christy. The street was empty except for a stray dog snuffling in the gutter for scraps.

After looking around to be sure she was alone, Molly knelt quickly in front of the door and stuck her finger into the large keyhole. She felt cold, sharp metal. That would be the first ward. Behind it was another ward. The wards didn't move; they were there to keep the wrong key from fitting into the lock. Behind the wards she felt the pin tumbler. The pin tumbler was the difficult part, because it turned. Any fool could pick a lock without a pin tumbler. But a pin-tumbler lock—for that you needed to be downy, with special skills and tools.

Molly went back to the house, picking up a few sticks from the woodpile on her way through the yard to explain her absence. She wondered if Mrs. Wilkes would be able to get a lockpick for her. They probably had such things at the Fool's Tavern.

On the other hand, involving Mrs. Wilkes might be expensive. After all, she would want her share. And Molly didn't actually need a fencing cull for this job. There wasn't much coin money used in New York, anyway, was there? And if the stuff on the Torah scrolls was pure silver, she ought to be able to trade it directly for passage on a ship. Especially if she hammered it about a bit first so that it wasn't quite so recognizable.

Still, a pin tumbler was a pin tumbler. How could you get past it without a real lockpick?

Molly mulled over the problem for several days. During the first two of those days, Christy lay on a pallet near the kitchen fire, and Mrs. Bell and Arabella cleaned her wounds frequently. Molly tried not to look at her. This was hard, because Molly seemed to be doing most of the housework, and generally it needed to be done in the kitchen.

This meant stepping around the pallet on the floor; and around Arabella and Mrs. Bell, who were tending Christy; and around the kittens and the cat. The cat walked right in front of Molly while she was carrying a bowl of milk to the table and stuck its fistlike head between her ankles. Molly tripped and fell. Milk and shards of broken bowl flew everywhere.

"Damn it to bloody hell!" Molly said.

"Molly!" said Mrs. Bell reprovingly.

The cat gave a summoning meow to her kittens,

who came waddling over to lap up the spilled milk. Rachel grabbed a kitten by the tail, and Molly, who was still lying flat on the floor, reached out and grabbed Rachel's wrist.

"I told you not to pull their bleedin' tails!" said Molly.

"Damn it to bloody hell!" Rachel said.

Christy noticed none of this. She hadn't spoken in the two days since she'd come to them. Sometimes her eyes opened, but they never seemed to focus. Or so Arabella and Mrs. Bell said. Molly avoided looking at Christy's face.

Christy's unconsciousness was a bad sign. It could mean brain fever had set in, Dr. Alvarez said, and that could be fatal.

On the third day, Christy began to moan and thrash about and to call out for her mother, who Arabella said was dead. Molly couldn't stand that. She ran from the room, and went upstairs and swept the bedrooms, which didn't need sweeping. Then she came downstairs and swept the parlor. Then she swept the stairs, and finally the front stoop.

But the following day, Christy began to speak sensibly, and Molly went back into the kitchen again. She had to—nobody else seemed to have any time for cooking, and yet the family had to eat. Mr. Bell and David couldn't be expected to help with it. It wasn't just that they didn't know how to do the things the women did, Molly thought; they didn't even know what those things were. It was lucky for the Bells that they had bought her, Molly thought with mingled pride and annoyance.

On the evening of the fourth day, Mr. Grant came to the door and demanded that Christy be sent back to him. Mr. Bell jumped up with his hot, angry look and spoke to him very sternly, mentioning the magistrate in spite of Arabella's begging him not to.

Molly wondered if Mr. Grant would come back with a constable and force the Bells to hand Christy over. But he didn't. Perhaps he realized that he had gone further than he ought to have in beating Christy. The colony had no law, of course, that he couldn't beat her; he could, as long as she didn't actually die. Sometimes it was hard to tell just what was allowed.

The puffs of yellow around Christy's wounds were supposed to be a very good sign. "Infection precedes healing," Dr. Alvarez said.

Molly chanced a look. She felt her stomach churn, and she had to run out of the kitchen again. That was a sure sign that she wasn't meant to grow up decent, Molly thought. Everyone else was trying to help Christy, which was a mitzvah, and Molly couldn't even stand to look at her.

Christy's eyes grew bright with fever. They moved her to the Dutch cabinet bed in the kitchen that

Arabella and Molly had shared, and Molly went on sleeping with Rachel at night, while Arabella took the pallet by the kitchen fire.

Cuddled beside Rachel at night in the trundle bed next to David's cot, Molly could hear Mr. and Mrs. Bell in the next room talking about what to do with Christy. They spoke very softly, and they must have thought no one could hear them, as older people often forget that children have sharper hearing.

"It's a mitzvah to take care of the sick," said Mrs. Bell. "But it would be a better mitzvah if we could buy her and get her away from that Grant creature."

"We can't afford her," said Mr. Bell. "And we don't need her, do we?"

"No," Mrs. Bell agreed. "I don't need any more help around the house. Really, we didn't need Molly either, of course."

"Well, that was a mitzvah too," said Mr. Bell. "Anyway, we can't buy Christy if Grant doesn't want to sell her, and why should he?"

"True," said Mrs. Bell, and she added something in Yiddish; Molly thought she was saying that you couldn't buy slaves in New York as easily as you once could.

Mr. Bell said something back in Yiddish. All Molly could understand of it was that it had something to do with stopping Mr. Grant from doing something—hurting Christy again, Molly supposed. She wondered whether the Bells might be able to buy Christy after

Molly ran away. Then they'd be performing a mitzvah by saving Christy from Grant, and Molly would be helping by running away. There was something wrong with that, but Molly couldn't think what. She wondered if David would understand that it was a mitzvah. Probably not.

"Even if he could be forced to sell her," said Mrs. Bell in English, "it might be that no one else would want to buy her. Because of 1712 and all."

"Yes, that's so," said Mr. Bell. "A lot of people are still frightened of another slave uprising. I suppose the worse they treat their own slaves, the worse they fear it."

"And we can't buy her," Mrs. Bell concluded. "So perhaps Arabella's right, and it's best to return Christy to Mr. Grant. After all, we're still paying for Molly, aren't we?"

"I had to take out a mortgage on my last shipment to Barbados to finish paying for her. If that ship comes in all right, she'll be paid for."

Molly was surprised at that. She thought Mr. Bell had bought her with money he just happened to have. Molly wasn't sure what a mortgage was, but it sounded like some sort of borrowed money. She wondered who Mr. Bell had borrowed the money from, and whether he would still have to pay off the mortgage after she had run away.

"Molly was an expensive mitzvah," Mrs. Bell mused. "But worth it. She's turning out better than we expected, isn't she?"

"She's certainly turning out to be more of a mitzvah than we expected," said Mr. Bell, and they both laughed softly. Molly didn't see the joke.

"Oh, it's just little things now and then, Ephraim," said Mrs. Bell. "Nothing worse than what our own children would do."

After that they switched to rapid Yiddish that Molly couldn't understand. She lay back and mused about the problem of the pin tumbler in the lock on the synagogue door. Nothing worse than their own children would do? David would never steal the silver from the ark. He probably didn't know how to pick even a simple lock. But it wasn't just that he couldn't. David wouldn't, of course. He was a bar mitzvah, a son of the law. Molly and the law had met only at the Old Bailey.

Molly shifted uncomfortably onto her side. The law mattered to David, more than going away into the wilderness and becoming a voyageur. And so did the Torah scrolls. The scrolls mattered to Mr. Bell, who had taken out a mortgage to keep her from being bought by people who poked her and looked at her teeth. And they mattered to Mrs. Bell, even though she never touched them or read from them—Mrs. Bell, who had never again tried to take away Molly's stockings, even though she did look at Molly's toes sticking through the holes in them and shake her head.

But then, Molly thought, she was just a mitzvah to the Bells. They might pretend to like her, but really they just wanted to think they were doing a good deed by buying her and making her work for them. Just as they were doing a good deed by taking care of Christy—a good deed that Molly couldn't stand to do.

She thought about Mr. Bell losing his temper and throwing Mr. Mendez's letter into the fire. Losing your temper wasn't really a mitzvah, but she still liked that he'd gotten so angry for her sake.

But she couldn't be their mitzvah. The mitzvah they wanted, she thought, was for her to grow up decent, as Captain Mattock had said. They wanted her to be a good Jewish girl, but she wasn't a good Jewish girl. She was a good pickpocket. And New York was no place for a pickpocket.

If only there were some way she could get back to London without taking the scrolls . . .

London—for some reason, the word didn't seem to have the magic warm sound of home that it had always had. She tried whispering it aloud, softly, but the only result was that Rachel rolled over in her sleep and punched Molly in the nose with her tiny fist. Molly lay awake for a long time, listening to the Bells whispering in Yiddish.

Thirteen

"There are four bodily humours," Dr. Alvarez explained. "Blood, phlegm, black bile, and yellow bile. Fever is caused when the humours become imbalanced."

"I thought it was from her wounds," said Arabella.

Molly was soaking a piece of meat from the shochet, the kosher butcher. Nobody seemed to notice that she was doing all of the cooking these days, and nobody had bothered to thank her. She didn't mind cooking, really. She had a good sense of what things to put together, and how to cook things to make them taste best. It probably came of having spent so much time thinking about food instead of eating it. She experimented with adding onions to things, or a little more salt, and most of the time everyone ate whatever she made without complaint—except for the time that she mistook soap flakes for sugar and added them to a hasty pudding for breakfast. She had decided she liked the odd-looking things called potatoes. The taste of them was thicker and more satisfying than that of turnips. The Bells would just have to get used to them.

Maybe when she got back to London, she'd be able to cook food sometimes, if she could find a way to build a decent fire.

"Yes, it's her wounds that caused the humours to become imbalanced," said Dr. Alvarez patiently. "That was from the shock, which we saw the night she was injured, when her pulse became rapid and faint. Now I must study her urine to find out which humour is imbalanced. Then we'll know whether to bleed her or purge her."

"Hasn't she bled quite enough already?" Mrs. Bell asked.

"Possibly. I'll know more after I study her urine."

Mrs. Bell and Arabella exchanged doubtful glances.

Molly picked up a pair of empty water buckets and a yoke to carry them with and started out the door.

"Molly, child, don't walk all the way out to the Tea Water Pump," said Mrs. Bell. "It's getting late. Buy some water from a water carrier at the market." She reached into her apron pocket, pulled out a string of sea-want, and handed it to Molly.

"She might get the Indian woman while she's out," Arabella suggested. "Rachel is outgrowing her moccasins."

Mrs. Bell looked at Arabella in surprise: "Goodness,

I didn't even notice! Molly, if Betty Moccasin is in the market, bespeak her for tomorrow."

Molly walked along Mill Street to the Old Slip Market by the East River. She found a water carrier there, a woman standing on a wagon loaded with barrels of water that was hitched to an old horse who smelled of sweat and flicked his ears at buzzing flies. Molly asked if the water was from the Tea Water Pump.

"Of course it is," said the woman irritably. "You think I'd try to poison people? Can't make a living that way."

Molly put her two buckets up on the wagon bed and held out the string of shell beads.

"Seawant?" said the woman. "Don't you have any real money?"

"This is what they gave me," said Molly, folding her arms on her chest. "Ma'am."

"I don't deal with bead-traders," said the woman, not reaching for the seawant. "Save that for the Indians."

Molly set the seawant down on the wagon bed. The woman lifted her foot as if to kick the beads off the wagon and into the dust.

Molly grabbed the woman's foot. "Keep your bleedin' dew-beater off my money or I'll stow your glim." Then, knowing that the Bells would want her to be polite, she added, "Please." She hoisted herself onto the wagon and dipped her buckets deep into an open barrel of clear water that reflected the sky above.

The woman glared at Molly, but picked up the sea-want and tucked it into a leather pocket she wore around her waist.

"Next time, bring English pennies," the woman called as Molly staggered heavily away.

Molly lugged the sloshing buckets back to the house and left them in the backyard. Then she went out again to look for Betty Moccasin, the Indian woman who had made her moccasins for her when she first arrived. Betty Moccasin wasn't in the Old Slip Market, or in the market by the harbor. Molly finally found her in White Hall, the square in front of Fort George. Betty agreed to come to the Bells' house in the morning.

From White Hall, Molly could see the waves breaking over the rocks at the water's edge, shooting white spray into the air. At the edge of White Hall, by the water just where the great boulders stopped, was Hunt's Shipyard. A ship was pulled up in dry dock there, looming overhead like an enormous misshapen house. The shipwrights were caulking the boards of the hull with oakum and with trowels laden with hot pitch. On the cobbles, a fire burned under a cauldron of pitch, keeping it bubbling hot and soft. When it cooled on the boards, it would dry sticky but quite hard, filling all the cracks in the ship's wooden hull and rendering it waterproof for a long time.

The smell of the bubbling hot pitch stayed with Molly as she walked slowly along the dock, back toward the market. She thought about the pin tumbler in the lock on the synagogue door.

In the market, the farmers and stallholders were packing up their wares. Molly's eyes fell on a cove who was taking apart a table, breaking it down into the boards and trestles to take home. He was a Dutch farmer, by the look of him, in buckskin breeches, a loose linen smock, and a blue broadcloth coat. The pocket of the coat bulged slightly, not enough to lift the flap but enough so that Molly could tell there was something in it. Molly watched the farmer closely, letting her eyelids droop as though she were looking at the ground. She tried to figure out what was in his pocket. A watch? A small purse?

It wasn't dark yet, and there was no close press of people to serve as a distraction or to hide what she did. And the pocket was the kind that usually didn't have a lining. The farmer bent down and hoisted two boards onto his shoulder. Molly sidled up to him and stood a little off to one side, pretending to be looking at the ships' masts outlined against the sunset. A seagull circled, cried out raucously, and landed on the top of a mast. The farmer carried the planks to the water's edge and lowered them down to a boat rocking in the water a few feet below. A woman standing in the boat reached up to take them.

The farmer turned and started back to get more boards. Molly took a few silent steps toward him. Then he stopped and reached into his pocket. He put his hand on the lump and drew it out. An apple. A stupid apple! And now his pocket was flat. Nothing but an apple.

He turned and held the apple out to Molly. *"Appel, meisje?"* he offered.

Molly reddened, annoyed and embarrassed. "No, thanks," she muttered.

She hadn't really been going to pick his pocket, anyway, she told herself. After all, she had a much bigger filch in mind. She turned and walked home in the dusk.

The next morning, Christy seemed somewhat better. Dr. Alvarez decided to bleed her four ounces just to be on the safe side. While he carefully laid out his lancet and a measuring bowl to catch the blood, and rolled up his sleeves, Betty Moccasin arrived to make Rachel's moccasins.

Rachel wouldn't take off her old moccasins until Molly took hers off too. Then Molly had to stand on the deerskin laid out on the floor so that Rachel would. She held Rachel still while Betty cut around Rachel's feet with a curved knife. Then Betty sat down on the settle by the fire, brought out a length of gut string, and began to stitch. Arabella brought some mending she was doing and sat down beside her, and they began to talk in low voices. It sounded to Molly as if they were speaking Dutch. Dutch was frustrating. If you just heard bits of it at a time, you could understand it—it was almost like

English. But the rapid stream of Dutch that Arabella and Betty Moccasin were muttering was incomprehensible. Molly noticed that the fire beneath the hasty pudding had burned too low, so she went outside in her stocking feet to get some firewood.

Mrs. Bell followed her out into the yard. "Molly, those stockings have become a disgrace," she said.

Molly looked down at the too-big stockings. She had darned them many times in the evenings while the family read and studied. But after a while, the stocking at the edges of the darn wore away and she had to darn between the darns. The holes in the bottoms kept getting bigger, and the runs up the sides, called louse-ladders, kept getting longer. There was almost as much darn as stocking now, and Molly felt the cold stones of the yard through the holes. She picked up a dry branch from the woodpile and smacked it against the flagstones, then knelt to gather up the fragments.

"They were my mother's," she said, without quite meaning to.

Mrs. Bell knelt beside Molly and swept up bits of wood with her hands. "Molly, tell me how your mother died."

Molly looked at Mrs. Bell, then picked at the wool on one of her stockings. She could feel it coming apart in her hands.

"Was it like Christy?" said Mrs. Bell gently.

"No. Yes. No, it wasn't." Molly swallowed. "The smallpox."

Mrs. Bell said, "The smallpox is terrible." She paused. "You had the smallpox too, didn't you, Molly?"

"Yes, but not then. Later. After Mama . . . I had it later."

Mrs. Bell was waiting, watching Molly, her eyes wanting to understand. But she couldn't, Molly knew. If Molly told her the truth, that kind expression would vanish. Mrs. Bell would send her away, send her out of her sight, maybe sell her.

"I had it after Mama d-died," Molly stammered. She hadn't used the word "died" before. Not about Mama and what had happened.

"Did you get it from her?"

"I guess," said Molly. That wasn't the important part.

"Who took care of you when you had it?"

"Nobody," said Molly. "I just had it, and we—I was there in the room for, I don't know, a long time and didn't know anything. Then I woke up one day and my mouth was all dry and I ran out of there and left he— left home." She was talking too fast, telling Mrs. Bell too much. "I mean, our room; that is, the room that Mama had off Cucumber Alley in Seven Dials. It was in a big house that had lots of rooms parted off with bits from packing crates, and the stairs had fallen down; you had to get up to our story by standing on a barrel. I just climbed down there and ran away and never went back."

Mrs. Bell was silent, letting her babble.

"Never," Molly repeated, as if explaining something important.

"How old were you?" Mrs. Bell was still looking at her, her eyes still sympathetic. That would change if she knew.

"Eight," Molly guessed.

"Who took care of your mother when she was sick, Molly?"

Molly looked at the gate leading out to the alley behind Mill Street. She *does* know, thought Molly. "I have to take this wood inside," she said. "The fire will burn out." She tried to stand up, but Mrs. Bell had ahold of her hand.

"The fire will burn out," Molly repeated. She tried again to stand up, but Mrs. Bell wouldn't move.

"Molly, who took care of your mother?"

"Nobody," said Molly. She felt her face burn. "I mean, I did, mostly I did. I tried; I couldn't . . ." Molly's throat closed up, and she couldn't speak. Suddenly it was very hard to breathe. She closed her eyes tightly. She pulled at one of her stockings and felt a darn tear apart.

She felt arms close around her, and she let Mrs. Bell hug her. Then she said the words that would make Mrs. Bell push her away, make her throw her down on the paving stones and order her to go away and never come back. "She got so bad," Molly whispered into Mrs. Bell's shoulder. "Her skin was all bumps—there wasn't any skin left, only great bubbling bumps on top of bumps, like Christy's skin that first night. And her eyes didn't see, and she only talked craziness, saying plaguey mad things. I knew she was going to . . . And I went to get the doctor. I left. And when I came back, she was . . ." Molly took a deep breath. "When I came back, she was dead."

Mrs. Bell must not have understood Molly, because she was still holding her, rocking her like a baby.

"I left her," Molly repeated, louder.

"To get the doctor. But you came back," said Mrs. Bell.

"When I came back, she was already . . ."

"Was the doctor with you?" Mrs. Bell asked.

"No," said Molly. They hadn't even let her in to see the doctor. The doctor's footman had jeered at her as she stood on the doctor's clean-scrubbed doorstep, barefoot and hardly coming up to his waist, with tear streaks cutting through the dirt on her face. The footman had tried to grab the gold sovereign she had in her hand too, but she'd been too quick for him. Looking back, she wondered where the gold sovereign had come from. If she'd ever stolen that much money, she'd have remembered it.

"The doctor wouldn't come," Molly explained. "So I went back and she was already dead."

"Oh, Molly," said Mrs. Bell.

"I shouldn't have left her," said Molly. It felt strange to be talking about it, just talking about it—to have said aloud what happened and to have the sun go on shining as it did before. "She was dying and I left her. And I was so scared." This was the part that she hated to tell, but it seemed as though it all had to come out now. "When I ran out to get the doctor, I think I was too scared to stay."

"You were only eight, Molly. God understands."

Molly was not interested in how God felt. "What about Mama?" she said.

"Your mama understands."

Molly thought it unlikely that Mrs. Bell would know how Mama felt. But she did feel better, oddly. She pulled away from Mrs. Bell and looked up at her.

Mrs. Bell pushed a stray lock of Molly's black hair away from her face. "And then you got sick? Who took care of you?"

"Nobody," said Molly. She remembered the days and nights of delirium lying on the bare boards of the cold room in Cucumber Alley, leaving the mattress to her mother, to what had been her mother. She remembered loud explosions and rats crawling over her, and spiders the size of dogs, and a coach-and-four charging across the room, driven by a skeleton in a purple velvet coat and knee breeches and a full-bottom wig. The doctor's footman kept offering her water to drink, and then pouring it on the ground and laughing maniacally while it turned into steaming blood. She remembered drinking all the beer in the pitcher and all the water in the bucket, slimy as it was, and being desperately thirsty, and she remembered cutting off her hair with the kitchen knife, as she had done for Mama—the kitchen knife Mama had chased Mr. Mendez with, getting up from her bed for the last time. And he had thrown the gold sovereign at Molly's feet before he ran out the door and fell down what should have been the stairs. That was where the money had come from. Mr. Mendez had been performing a mitzvah, visiting the sick. Trying to, anyway.

"Nobody? Molly, how could you survive the smallpox with no one to take care of you?"

Molly shrugged. She didn't know how. She'd just done it.

"And what happened to you after you got better?" asked Mrs. Bell.

"I just left, like I told you. And I went out and joined up with . . . with some people," she finished lamely.

"Some thieves?" said Mrs. Bell. "A thieves' den?"

Molly nodded. There had been many different places and many different people. Not all of them were thieves. Some of them did other things, things Molly was sure Mrs. Bell didn't know about and wouldn't understand. Molly had never stayed with any of them very long. She couldn't remember now all the places she'd been, or how long she'd stayed in any of them.

"And who buried your mother?" said Mrs. Bell.

Molly shrugged again. "No one. I left her there."

Now Mrs. Bell did look surprised, just for a moment, though Molly saw her hide her reaction quickly. "You mean you left . . . you left her body in the room? Without telling anybody? Without doing anything?"

"Well, yes," said Molly. "It didn't matter."

Mrs. Bell was staring at her now. She didn't understand.

"I mean that in London it doesn't matter," Molly explained. "There are dead people all over the place, I mean. You see people in the street that have died from gin, or from being cold, or babies that somebody just left there . . ." She trailed off. She wasn't getting the words right, couldn't find a way to explain that in London one more dead poor person didn't matter. And she could see that Mrs. Bell really didn't understand. Molly looked at the doorway to the alley again.

David was standing there. Their eyes met. Mrs. Bell looked up, saw him too, and made a gesture for him to go away. But David didn't go away. He came into the yard and knelt down beside them.

"Molly, did anyone say the Mourner's Kaddish for your mother?" he asked.

Mrs. Bell looked surprised. "But it's been more than eleven months since Molly's mother died, David. It's been two years."

"But I can still say the Kaddish for her," David said stubbornly. "If nobody else has."

"What's the Kaddish?" said Molly.

"The mourner's prayer," said Mrs. Bell. "You've seen the men say it in the synagogue and step backward. Each of them is saying it for somebody who died."

"I'm going to say it. I'll say it every morning in the synagogue for eleven months," David said. "For your mother." Mrs. Bell nodded approvingly.

Molly looked at them both looking at her, one pair of blue eyes and one pair of black. They seemed so sure that saying the mourner's prayer for Molly's mother would make things better. But Molly knew there was no way she could change the fact that she'd run out to get the rich doctor—who she must have known wouldn't come, anyway, wouldn't drive his precious carriage into Seven Dials, wouldn't stand on the old barrel to climb up to Molly's mother's room. Even though she knew nothing could change what had happened, still, Molly felt better.

Molly realized her face was wet. She was ashamed of what Mrs. Bell and David must think of her, crying like a baby. She wiped her nose on her apron, gathered up an armload of sticks without looking at them, and went back into the house.

After Dr. Alvarez bled Christy, she began to get better. The feverish brightness left her eyes, and her skin was no longer hot to the touch. In a few more days, Christy got up on wobbly legs and pulled on an old dress of Mrs. Bell's. Her own clothes had been torn to shreds by Mr. Grant's whip.

"I can't thank you enough," she said to Mrs. Bell. "I'll return the dress when I can."

"You're not leaving already?" said Mrs. Bell. Christy's skin was still a mass of scabs and welts.

"He'll want me back." Christy glanced nervously at the back door, as though Mr. Grant were standing behind it.

"Not yet, surely," said Mrs. Bell. "You could stay a couple days longer."

"He wouldn't like that," said Christy, again looking at the door.

"He'd be angry," said Arabella. "Christy had better go home now."

Mrs. Bell looked helplessly from one to the other. Molly thought she was wishing Mr. Bell were there to help her argue. But Mr. Bell and David had already gone to the warehouse on Dock Street. Molly couldn't understand why Christy was in such a hurry to go back to Mr. Grant, but she must know him better than Mrs. Bell did.

Again Molly wondered whether the Bells would be able to buy Christy after she ran away. For some reason, the thought made her feel heavy and sad. She tried to think of London, but pictures of New York kept coming into her head instead. Of Arabella and Mrs. Bell patiently showing her how to make her letters in the sand. Of David up in a tree, telling her that she belonged. Of the newborn kittens on the piled ropes at the warehouse. Of Rachel clinging everlastingly to Molly's skirts.

So Christy left, with Arabella standing at the door, watching after her anxiously, and Mrs. Bell murmuring a prayer for Christy under her breath.

Molly gathered up the breakfast dishes to wash in the yard. As she filled the wooden tub with water, she carefully slipped one of the pewter spoons into her pocket. She knew how to make a key for picking locks from a spoon, although she had never actually done it herself.

She worked on the spoon for most of the day, when she had a chance between chores and errands and when no one was watching her. It was an ordinary spoon, made of leaden pewter. The bowl was perfectly round, like a tiny soup bowl, and the handle was a long, thin stick of metal. She jammed the handle into the earth between two paving bricks until only the bowl was above ground. She used the head of the ax the Bells used to chop firewood to beat the bowl until it was folded in half. Then she pounded it thinner. When she was done, she had a piece of metal shaped like a capital letter *T*. With a little wriggling, she should be able to slip it past the wards in a lock and use it to turn the bolt. But not by holding on to the spoon's stick-shaped handle: the bolt might be hard to turn. So she made a crosswise handle out of a stick of kindling wood, boring a hole through it with the point of a nail. Now she would have enough leverage to turn her makeshift key. All she had to do was figure out how to deal with the pin tumbler.

Molly rehearsed picking the lock in her mind. But her brain wanted to skip around the part where she actually took the silver, which was odd because that should have been the most interesting part. She thought about picking the lock, and then about going home— "home" meaning London-home, of course. For some reason, she found herself thinking of Captain Mattock's parting words: "Go home, grow up decent, and don't hang."

Molly didn't have any intention of hanging. But she did mean to get home.

Fourteen

It was Friday night. Mr. Bell and David had gone to the synagogue. Mrs. Bell had just lit the Sabbath candles on the table and was covering her eyes to say the Sabbath prayer. Molly slipped out the kitchen door. She stole across the yard, her feet in their deerskin moccasins making hardly any noise on the paving stones.

Gathering her skirts in her hands, she slipped into the yard of the house behind the Bells', then around that house into Duke Street. She ran down Duke Street to Broad Street, and down Broad Street to the docks. She made her way quickly past the dark docks, hoping that René Duguay was somewhere far away. She saw only a few people, and most of them were engaged in putting away their work for the evening. She crossed the pier to the shipyard at the edge of White Hall.

The ship in dry dock loomed hugely against the

darkening sky, looking like the ghost of an ancient ship-wreck. Its bowsprit leaned overhead, and for a moment Molly had the illusion that the whole ship was about to come crashing down on her. Beside it the ribs of a long-boat stood out from the shadows like the skeleton of some antediluvian beast.

The shipwrights had gone home. The fire under the cauldron of pitch had died down to a few embers glowing in the night. Molly picked her way through the scattered scraps of lumber on the cobbles and touched the cauldron's iron side. It was still warm. Standing in the pitch was the stick used to stir it.

Molly drew the stick out. It emerged slowly, carrying a goopy glop of black pitch with it. Molly turned the stick slowly and watched the threads of pitch wrap around it.

"Hey, you!" a man's voice cried. "Get away from there!"

Molly didn't turn to see who had yelled at her. She ran, holding the stick in front of her, her moccasins pattering lightly and swiftly over the cobbles. Moccasins were much better for running away in than clogs were. She ran back through the docks and up Broad Street to Mill Street.

She stopped in front of the synagogue. The man from the shipyard hadn't bothered to chase her. There was nobody about, Molly thought. A lot of the people who lived on Mill Street were Jews, and they were all at home now, since the Sabbath had begun. Molly squelched an odd little feeling that she should be home too. Well, she'd get this done quickly. She glanced around once and then slid through shadows up to the synagogue's main door.

She bent over and looked into the keyhole. It was big, like the key that fit it. Molly could put her finger into it. She felt the two wards, which didn't move, and behind the wards she felt the pin tumbler. The pin tumbler was the difficult part. With the pitch, maybe she could stop the pin tumbler from turning. Then the lock would be easy to pick, like the plain ward lock on the women's door.

Molly had never heard of anyone stopping a pin tumbler with pitch to pick a lock, but it seemed to make sense to her.

She took a long straw that she had pulled from the broom in the kitchen. She got a nice glop of pitch onto the end of it.

She peered into the keyhole. It was dark in there; you couldn't see a thing. Well, the pin tumbler would be behind the wards, and as long as she stuck the straw straight in, it shouldn't touch them.

She knelt down and carefully pushed the straw into the keyhole until she felt it hit the pin tumbler. Then she wiggled it around, spreading the pitch. When she drew the straw out, the pitch was almost all gone from the end.

Perfect.

Now she just needed to let the pitch set for a few hours and the pin tumbler would be firmly glued in place. That should do the trick.

Molly rose and moved quickly and quietly through the shadows of the houses on Mill Street, tossing the pitch-covered stick over a fence into a yard as she went. She didn't look back; if she had, she might have seen Hesper Crudge standing at the corner of Mill Street, watching her with a satisfied smirk.

Molly got home just in time for a quiet dinner. Everyone seemed tired, and they went to bed early. Although Christy had gone home to Mr. Grant, Molly was still sharing little Rachel's bed upstairs, as Rachel insisted. Molly slipped off her moccasins and slid into bed in the dark, leaving her dress on over her shift. She lay still and listened for the Bells' breathing next door to become even. Mr. Bell began to snore. Time went by.

At last everyone seemed to be asleep—Mr. and Mrs. Bell, and David and Rachel. Molly lifted the blankets and slid out of the trundle bed sideways, easing her feet carefully onto the floor. She picked up her moccasins and felt in her pocket for the key she'd made out of the pewter spoon. She took a step. A floorboard creaked. She stopped and listened. Mr. Bell was still snoring.

She took another step. Waited, listened. Another. And another. The floor creaked again.

Mrs. Bell rolled over and coughed. Molly froze.

"Don't put so much wood on the fire, dear," said Mrs. Bell. "You'll smother the kittens."

She was talking in her sleep. Molly took another step.

Finally, she reached the top of the stairs and started down. She kept to the edge of the stairs so they wouldn't creak, putting both feet on each step before moving to the next one.

At the bottom of the stairs, she stopped and listened again. Then she began to creep along the hall toward the door. She almost tripped over the mother cat, who gave a little meow and rubbed her flank against Molly's leg. Molly reached down and stroked the cat's ears.

The key wasn't in the keyhole. The door would be locked, Molly knew, and door locks couldn't be opened from either side without a key. Picking the lock would make too much noise.

Surely the key must be in the kitchen door. Molly crept back along the hall and pushed open the door to the kitchen.

Arabella and Christy stared at her in the light of a beeswax candle.

She stared at them.

Christy was supposed to be back home, with Mr. Grant. But she wasn't. She was there in the kitchen, wrapped in a woolen travel cloak. Christy was watching Arabella, who was frozen in the act of slicing a wedge off a wheel of cheese.

Nobody said anything for a moment.

Then Arabella said tensely, "Why are you up?"

"What is she doing here?" said Molly. But her mind was working ahead. "Where are you sending her? Where is she going?"

Arabella took a step toward her, still holding the knife in her hand. "Go back to bed, Molly. You haven't seen anything."

"That's why Christy had to go home," Molly said. They were both speaking in whispers, but their whispers sounded loud in the silent house. "So that the Bells wouldn't be suspected when she ran away."

Christy drew her breath in sharply between her teeth. Arabella gestured meaningfully with the knife and snapped, "Shut up, Molly!"

Molly stepped backward, her hands fumbling for a weapon. They closed around the empty iron kettle on the hearth. She heaved it up and managed to hold it unsteadily in front of her. Some weapon. She couldn't even swing it.

"You back off and stow that chiff," she said, putting all the menace she could into her voice.

Arabella looked at the pot and smiled slightly. "Molly, put that stupid thing down."

"Put the knife down," said Molly.

"She isn't going to do anything, Arabella," Christy whispered. "These are good folk in this house. Do put that knife down."

"You don't know this one like I do," said Arabella harshly. "She's a London convict. She'd do anything if she thought it would get her something."

"I would not!" said Molly, offended. How could Arabella think that of her? "I never sang out beef on anyone in my life! You don't know me at all if that's what you think." She angrily set the pot down on the brick floor with a clang that rang through the night-hushed house.

"Quiet!" Arabella said, belatedly.

Molly looked at Christy, who watched her in silence through still-swollen eyelids. "I wouldn't," said Molly vehemently. She couldn't believe that anybody would think such a thing of her. As if she were no different from Hesper Crudge. "I wouldn't gab to anyone. I know you have to get away, Christy. I can see what's right in front of my own eyes."

"That's a wonder, when you're so wrapped up in yourself all the time," Arabella muttered.

Molly was about to reply indignantly, but Christy interrupted. "I believe her, Arabella," said Christy. She reached out, took the knife from Arabella's hand, and quietly started cutting boiled beef with it.

Arabella turned around and scowled at Christy.

"That's a cheese knife!" She grabbed the knife out of Christy's hand. "Now we're going to have to boil it. Molly, go find me another knife."

Molly thought of refusing, because she was angry at Arabella for thinking that she, Molly, was no better than Hesper Crudge. But she also felt relieved to be trusted. And she wanted to help Christy escape from Mr. Grant; that was a mitzvah she could handle. She was *not* all wrapped up in herself, and Arabella had no business saying so. She went into the pantry and brought out another knife.

"Where are you sending her? Is she going to England?" Molly's voice caught on the last word.

"There's slavery in England too," said Arabella.

"Then where?" she asked.

Arabella sighed. "To the Mohawks," she said grudgingly.

"The Mohocks?" Molly spoke loudly in her surprise. The only Mohocks she knew of were the gang of wealthy footpads in London. Christy might as well stay with Mr. Grant as go to them.

"Hush!" said Arabella. "Get me one of the blankets from the cabinet bed, and then go find some rope to make a bundle."

Molly did what Arabella had asked. As they rolled the bundle together on the floor, there came a scratching at the kitchen door. Arabella nodded to Molly to open it.

Betty Moccasin came in. She looked at Molly and then cast a questioning glance at Arabella.

"It's all right," said Arabella. "She won't talk."

"Hurry up," said Betty shortly.

"We're ready," said Arabella. Christy pursed her lips and nodded.

"Molly," said Arabella, "stay here and lock the door after we're gone. Then wait up till I come back. And if you say anything to anybody about this . . ."

"Where are you going?" asked Molly.

"The less you know, the better," snapped Arabella. Then she added, more gently, "Someday maybe I'll tell you. But I'll be gone an hour, two at the most."

"All right," said Molly. She wondered if she could get the synagogue job done in an hour. She would have to—there wouldn't be another chance. The pitch in the lock would surely be noticed in the morning.

Arabella turned the key in the kitchen door, and drew it out of the lock. She opened the door just a crack. Christy tucked her bundle under her cloak. Betty Moccasin slipped sideways through the narrow opening.

A moment later, she was back. "Someone is out there," Betty said. "Someone is watching us."

Fifteen

"**Is it Grant?**" Arabella asked. "Would he miss you already, Christy?"

"He was dead drunk," said Christy. "He won't come out of it till morning, and then he'll be sick with the headache all day."

"Somebody small," said Betty. "A child, a small woman. But no one followed me."

"I'll go see," said Arabella.

"No!" said Molly, startled. She thought they should all stay in the kitchen. Anything else was crazy. Why go out if they were being watched? Her thoughts raced down twisting London alleys where coves with knives lurked in the shadows.

"I'll go to the jakes," said Arabella. "And I'll see what I can see."

Arabella had sharper eyes than Molly, especially in

the dark. Molly opened the door a crack and Arabella slipped out. Molly heard her footsteps cross the yard, and then heard the door of the privy open and close.

A few minutes later, Arabella was back. "It's a girl," she said. "I think it's that ragged girl that came in on the same ship as Molly."

"Hesper Crudge," Molly breathed.

"What are we going to do now?" said Christy. "I can't stay here all night."

Hesper must have seen Molly working on the lock at the synagogue. It was Molly she was waiting for; Molly was sure of it.

Molly took a deep breath. She felt the T-shaped key in her pocket. She thought about the silver in the synagogue, and the four pounds she hoped it was worth. She thought about passage back to England. London.

Then she thought of Christy's face the night that Mr. Grant beat her.

Molly tried to get the thought of London back, but it wouldn't come. Christy's swollen, bleeding face was in her mind instead. Then, when the image of London came back to her, it seemed all bloody too. She remembered people fighting, beating each other; she remembered an execution she had gone to at Tyburn where nine people were hanged at once, all wearing burial shrouds like long white nightgowns.

Molly hadn't told Arabella what she was doing out

of bed. It wouldn't occur to Arabella that Molly was running away. With a funny twist in her stomach, Molly suddenly saw her situation through Arabella's eyes. Molly had no reason to run away. The Bells were kind to her. Kind to her and Arabella both, really. But the Bells owned Molly only until she was twenty-one. They owned Arabella for the rest of her life. What was it Arabella had said? *Until the grave set her free.*

Molly looked at Christy's face, at the long scabs that still crisscrossed her cheeks. One of them ended at the corner of her left eye. The grave had almost set Christy free already. And it would soon, if she stayed. What Mr. Grant hadn't managed to do this time, he would do next time, or the time after that.

Molly felt for the key in her pocket again. She wasn't going to steal the silver from the synagogue. She was going to help Christy, to help Arabella set her free before the grave. She wasn't going to steal any silver, and she wasn't going to go to London. She was going to stay with the Bells, here in this little brick house on Mill Street near the synagogue. Until she reached the age of twenty-one, as her indenture said. She tried to feel disappointed, but instead she felt as if a great weight had lifted from her shoulders.

This was what she wanted. Maybe she'd wanted it for a long time, at least with part of her mind—the part that wasn't figuring out how to make a key and how to pick the lock. Long ago she had belonged to Mama, and now she belonged here. Belonging to people was just the way things were.

"I'll go out," she said. "Hesper will follow me."

The others looked at her. "How do you know?" said Arabella.

"Because," said Molly, "she wants to snabble me, to catch me at something. She wants to make trouble for me. She has, ever since we were on the ship. She's like that." Molly dropped her moccasins on the floor and stepped into them. "Wait here a few minutes," she said. "I'll lead her up Mill Street, toward the synagogue. Then you two go toward the Old Slip Market. I'll keep her busy as long as I can."

Arabella frowned. "What if she tries to hurt you?"

"Then I'll sing out bloody murther if I have to," said Molly. "But I don't think that's what she'll do." Not if I give her something really interesting to watch, she added to herself.

"Well, all right," said Arabella reluctantly. "I'll take the key. If you get back before me, wait in the yard."

Christy looked at Molly. "Thank you," she whispered.

Molly slipped out into the dark yard, then through the narrow space between the houses to Mill Street. She moved along the cobbled pavement quietly in her moccasins. She sensed rather than heard Hesper Crudge following her. Hesper must have taken off her clogs and been carrying them in her hands. Or maybe the clogs didn't even fit anymore. Molly hoped Hesper wasn't going to jump on her, hoped she didn't have a knife. Molly should have brought one. Her heart beat fast, but she tried to look like she was just sneaking along the street unawares. It was hard to look like you didn't know you were being followed when you did know.

Molly came to the synagogue. She made a show of looking up and down Mill Street, and even looked in the direction from which she knew Hesper must be watching. She couldn't see her; Molly's eyes had never been very sharp except close up, anyway.

Then Molly knelt in front of the main door, the men's door, and drew out the key made from the pewter spoon. She inserted the T-shaped end into the keyhole and wriggled it carefully past the wards. She poked it around until she felt the bit catch in the latch. She turned the key.

And nothing happened.

Molly turned the key again, as hard as she could, using the wooden lever that she'd made. Again, nothing happened.

The pitch had set in the pin tumbler, and it had frozen the lock fast.

Well, that was a problem. Molly sat back on her heels. Definitely a problem. In fact, there was no way she could get to the main floor of the synagogue. And how long could she keep Hesper distracted if she didn't?

Maybe if she broke a window . . . ?

But Molly rejected that idea instantly. The noise would bring someone running, or Hesper would sound the alarm. And then Christy might get caught.

The important thing was to keep Hesper watching her for as long as possible. Long enough for Christy to get completely away.

Molly went over to the women's door. She took out her makeshift key and slid it past the wards, then hooked the latch and heard the lock pop open with a gentle click.

Molly pulled the door open. She closed it behind her, but not quite all the way, and then felt her way up the stairs to the women's balcony.

Standing by the railing, she looked through the lattice to the floor below. On the east wall, the eternal flame burned in its glass holder, throwing enough light to show the outline of a chandelier and the doors to the ark beneath that held the Torah scrolls. She saw the polished gleam of the wooden railing that surrounded the ark. The rest of the synagogue was in total darkness.

Molly heard the barely perceptible creak of a footstep on the stairs.

Hesper was coming up. She wouldn't know there was nothing to steal up there. She was coming to watch Molly steal so that she could give evidence against her, as she'd boasted about doing against her gang members.

She probably wanted to see Molly hang, or at least get whipped at the whipping post. Well, too bad. She was going to be disappointed.

But the longer Molly could keep her up here, the better it would be for Christy. Arabella hadn't told Molly where she and Betty Moccasin were taking Christy, but with water surrounding the tiny city on three sides, Molly could guess that they were taking a boat. Molly didn't know what other helpers they had, or what steps they'd taken not to be seen. But her part was to keep Hesper off the streets and out of their way. She decided to make Hesper waste time looking for her. The balcony was three-sided, shaped like a U with the stairs at the bottom. Molly took her moccasins off and held them in her hands. She crept toward the near end of the U, as far away from the stairs as she could get.

She could barely make out Hesper emerging from the stairs. Molly watched as Hesper stood still and waited for her eyes to become accustomed to the dark. Then Hesper crept forward, toward the glow of the eternal flame. The lattice stopped her. Molly watched as Hesper stared down into the darkness, her fingers laced through the lattice as though she were clutching the bars of a prison cell. Hesper must be wondering where Molly was. Then Hesper began to move along the railing, feeling her way.

She's not looking for me anymore, she's looking

for a way down, Molly realized. She wants to get down to the ark. How does she know?

London thieves' instinct, Molly answered herself. There was nothing to steal up here, so it must be down there. She stood still and silent while Hesper worked her way around the balcony near the lattice. Well, let her search, thought Molly. There aren't any stairs down into the synagogue. And this will give Christy more time.

Now and then, Molly heard Hesper's bare feet brush the floor. Hesper didn't move nearly quietly enough for a thief. Molly could have taught her a thing or two.

Molly was sitting on a bench, pressing herself into the corner of the wall. Her muscles were beginning to ache from not moving. Should she move and let Hesper see her? No, not yet; not until Hesper decided to give up. Now Hesper was working her way along the benches. Silently, Molly slipped onto the floor and slid under the bench.

Molly could leave now, run down the stairs, and lock the door behind her. That would take care of Hesper. But no; it would be too hard to explain to everyone the next morning why Hesper was locked in the synagogue. Especially when Hesper told her version of the story. It was better to just . . .

Molly was startled out of her thoughts by the crack of splitting wood. She peered out from under the bench. Hesper had worked a section of the lattice loose from the railing and had lifted it down. Molly rose to her feet and watched in disbelief as Hesper, in the glow from the eternal flame, climbed over the railing, hung by her hands, and dropped to the floor below.

That wasn't fair! This was Molly's theft; she had planned it carefully. And now she'd nobly given it up in order to help Christy. There was no way she was going to let Hesper get it instead.

Molly looked over the railing. It seemed a long way down. She set her moccasins down, climbed over the railing, and hung by her hands, then by her fingertips, her legs and her long skirts swinging. She closed her eyes tightly and let go.

When Molly hit the floor, pain shot up through the soles of her feet all the way to her teeth. She reeled backward. In the same instant, Hesper Crudge was on top of her, punching her in the stomach and the face. Molly drew up her legs and pushed Hesper off of her with both feet and her hands. Then she scrambled to her feet and faced Hesper, fists raised.

Hesper sneered, but under the sneer she looked frightened. Molly realized for the first time that Hesper wasn't as big as Molly anymore.

Hesper glanced behind her at the dark shape of the reading desk. It was raised on a dais, surrounded by a railing. Hesper must think whatever was worth stealing was in there, Molly realized. Under its cloth cover, the desk did look as if it could be a chest holding something of value. Her fists still raised, Molly sidestepped her way between Hesper and the dais, her back to the reading desk.

Molly and Hesper faced each other for a moment, their eyes darting to catch the other's slightest move.

"I'll go halves with you," Hesper said.

"I'll see you hanged first," said Molly.

Hesper snickered. "You bleedin' well owe me. Ended up in a bob-ken with nib folks, didn't you?"

Molly stared at Hesper. Suddenly she had a vision of the night she'd been caught in London. Those two nib culls grabbing her, and the old constable holding up the lantern. Someone dodging away from the light, slipping into the darkness. A quick swish of ragged skirts, a bedraggled colorless dress hanging over the skinny, too-small frame of a ragged London pickpocket like herself.

"You." Molly looked at Hesper. "You shopped me."

Hesper shrugged. "Maybe."

Molly thought fast. She'd always known who Hesper was, because Hesper was famous on the canting lay. Famous for shopping people. But she'd never met Hesper before her sentencing. "But how? You didn't even know me."

"Know everyone, don't I?" Hesper took a step backward, fists raised, not taking her eyes off Molly. "It's my business to know everyone. Turn 'em in, don't I?"

"For blood money." Molly took a step toward Hesper.

Hesper sneered. "I never got no bleedin' blood money. Bleedin' judges never hanged no one I turned in." She spat sideways on the floor in disgust, still not taking her eyes off Molly. "Transported 'em all. So I ain't never got no forty pounds."

"You would kill someone for forty pounds." You'd kill *me* for forty pounds, Molly thought, but somehow she didn't feel like saying it. It gave her a hollow feeling, knowing that Hesper had tried to get her scragged. But it didn't really surprise her. In a funny way, she almost understood.

"Cor, I'd do it for less than that," said Hesper, grinning. "Wouldn't be me that killed 'em, anyway; be Jack Ketch. Don't see how you're any different from me. Do anything for money, wouldn't we?"

"No," said Molly uncomfortably, thinking of the silver in the ark. The thought made her stomach hurt, and she wished she'd never seen the plaguey silver. "No," she said more firmly. "I . . ." Then she stopped, her London instincts alerted. "You're packing a chiff! Drop it."

In answer, Hesper whipped a glinting blade from under her apron and drove it at Molly's stomach. Molly sidestepped quickly, grabbing Hesper and throwing her to the floor. Molly landed on top of Hesper. Hesper still gripped the knife tightly in her fist, and Molly, on top of her, had to clutch Hesper's wrist in both hands to keep her from using it. Hesper rolled and squirmed under her. Molly bit Hesper's arm hard and jerked the blade away from her. It wasn't a knife, she saw; it was a gleaming, sharp, jagged chunk of stone. Molly reared back and threw the stone, as hard as she could, at the open space over the women's balcony where Hesper had taken the lattice out. She couldn't see where the rock actually went, but she heard a crash of broken glass that might have been a lamp or a windowpane. At the same moment, Hesper punched her in the nose with all her strength. Molly fell backward, and Hesper dealt her a passing kick before she vaulted over the rail surrounding the reading desk. Molly scrambled to her feet and climbed over the rail after Hesper, landing on top of her as they both fell against the desk, which tipped over and hit the railing with a splintering crack.

Molly had a vision of Mr. Bell, his eyes flashing with anger.

Hesper struggled to her feet. "Bleedin' hell! I said I'd go halves."

"And I said . . . ," Molly began.

A key rattled in the lock of the main door. "Something's wrong with this lock," a man said in a muffled voice. "The key won't turn."

Molly and Hesper stopped struggling and stared at each other. Molly hadn't noticed the growing daylight till now. She could see Hesper's narrowed eyes and cutthroat's face clearly.

"Let me try," said another voice.

"Is there a bleedin' bolt-hole out of this crib?" asked Hesper.

Molly pointed up at the balcony, at the gap in the lattice where they'd dropped down. It was at least ten feet above their heads.

Hesper cursed. "Where's that go?" she asked, pointing to the double doors of the ark.

It did look like a doorway.

"I don't know," said Molly.

Hesper dashed up the steps to the ark and tried to yank the doors open, but they wouldn't budge. Ha! Locked as well, Molly thought with satisfaction.

"How are we supposed to get out?" Hesper said.

"Well, it was your plaguey cork-brained idea to come down here," Molly whispered. "This is an autem-ken, not a bleedin' gin shop. It don't have no bolt-holes."

The key rattled in the lock again. Molly heard several voices now, murmuring on the other side of the door. She glanced at the colored-glass windows just as the outline of a head appeared at one of them.

"Get down!" she hissed. But Hesper was already crouching in the shadows.

More heads showed dimly through the windows. Molly looked at the windows opposite the door. Could she open one of them? One had a latch. She crept toward it, staying in the long shadows, staying near the floor.

"What's going on? Is there someone inside?" said one of the men at the window.

Molly stood up slowly, reaching for the window latch.

"I can't see a thing," another man said. "But I thought I heard voices in there."

A man said something in Portuguese. Molly stretched upward, and her fingers just brushed the latch.

Hesper was beside her. "Give me a leg up."

Molly bent over and made a step with her hands, and Hesper put one bare foot into it.

Hesper reached for the latch, almost turned it, and then lost her balance and fell. Footsteps pounded up the stairs to the women's gallery.

Molly boosted Hesper up again. Hesper swayed, caught the latch with her fingers, turned it, and pulled the window open. Then she vaulted over the windowsill and was gone without giving Molly a backward glance.

"There's someone inside. I can hear them," a man's voice said from the stairs.

Molly reached up and gripped the window ledge with her hands. She tried to pull herself up, but her hands slipped and she fell back to the floor. Her palms were slick with sweat. Frantically, she wiped them dry on her apron, took a few paces back, and made a running jump at the window. She grabbed the windowsill and climbed desperately, her stockinged toes scrabbling at the wall.

She swung over the windowsill and landed on all

fours in the yard below. She started running before she was fully upright—running as she had run in London, running for her life. She stumbled out of the synagogue yard and into an alley, then dodged into another alley. She couldn't see Hesper anywhere. How nice it would be to never see Hesper again. But she would, she was sure of it.

When Molly came to Broad Street, she stopped running. No one was chasing her. She stepped out of the alley into the cold muck that covered the cobbled street and felt it squish up between her toes. She looked down in surprise. She'd left her moccasins in the synagogue. She hoped no one would notice them. She was sure someone would. She reached down and pulled off her muddy stockings.

She thought of Hesper scurrying off without even looking back, without even wondering if Molly would be able to get out the window. Hesper, who would sell Molly's life—would sell anybody's—for less than forty pounds. That was the way things had really been back in London, most of the time. In Molly's London, anyway— an all-out fight for survival in which you couldn't be bothered to think about other people. But Molly wasn't like that. Molly cared about other people. Of course she did! It was completely unfair of Arabella to think that she didn't. All wrapped up in herself? Hmph.

And for Hesper to say Molly would do anything for

money! Molly had never called the bleedin' constables on anybody in her life.

Molly kept walking, away from the synagogue, away from Mill Street. She wandered down Broad Street in the chilly gray dawn. The night was over. Christy must have gotten away by now. Probably Arabella was back home, stirring the fire and putting on water to boil and doing the other things that Mrs. Bell and Molly couldn't do because it was the Jewish Sabbath. Perhaps she was wondering where Molly was.

Molly needed time to think.

She walked down the wide street, between the stair-stepped gables of tall brick and stone houses. A pig that had forgotten to go home the night before rooted through a pile of refuse in the gutter. A cat slunk through the shadows, intent on troubles of its own.

When Molly reached the harbor, it was light enough to see the black forest of masts and yardarms of the ships at port. Molly didn't think about where those sleeping ships were going. They were in New York for now, and so was she. She crossed the silent square by the docks where the market was held. A few rotting cabbage leaves clung to the cobbles, and a tattered *New York Gazette* stirred slightly in a dawn breeze.

She crossed the dock where she had fallen on the day that Mr. Bell bought her. The dock where Rachel hadn't drowned and where Mrs. Wilkes and Christy and everybody else had helped to find her. She walked along the dock to White Hall, and then out to the end of the quay. She looked back at the star-shaped Fort George rising behind her, and then out at the water. Waves crashed against the rocks beyond the quay, splattering her with cold droplets.

She looked at the pink wash of the eastern sky. A seagull took flight from the dock and flew in a wide circle before the rising sun.

England was that way. Somewhere out there, beyond the pink, Mr. Mendez had visited her in Newgate and kind Mr. Lopez had given her an orange. Somewhere out there the judge had come within a hairbreadth of hanging her for stealing something—she still wasn't sure what. Had it been the watch from that satin-coated cove in Mayfair? Or the purse with two silver half crowns and a banknote that turned out to be counterfeit? Or something else she couldn't remember? It didn't matter now.

And somewhere out there, Darby Mattock was bullying another load of captives bound for this new land. A land with plenty to eat and not much money, where someone would buy them and own them for years.

It occurred to Molly that she was actually freer than she had been before she belonged to the Bells.

The Bells. Molly sighed and looked down at the waves crashing beneath her feet. Mr. Bell was going to be angry. And Mrs. Bell was going to be disappointed.

And David . . . well, Molly didn't even want to think about what David would think. Molly needed to come up with a good story to explain what had happened last night. She thought briefly of telling the truth—except about Christy, of course. But the truth was complicated. Maybe you had to be a pickpocket to understand how something could be against the law and still be a mitzvah.

Well, whatever happened, it would pass. And she would still be here, and she would still belong.

Molly looked out at the water. To her left was the East River; to her right Hudson's River. Ahead were the Narrows, which were part of the sea that reached to England, to London.

And somewhere, on one of those rivers, a boat was rowing Christy to freedom.

Molly took the key from her pocket and turned it over in her hands. The first rays of dawn caught the jagged edges of metal as she flung it into the sea.

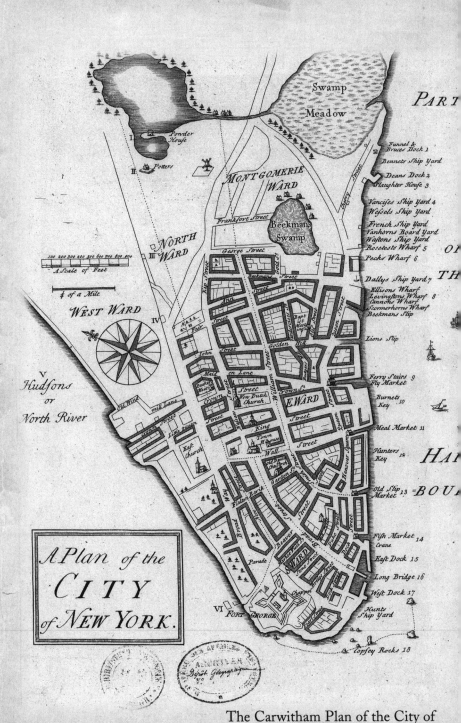

The Carwitham Plan of the City of
New York depicts the city circa 1730.

How Much of This Story Is True?

A few of the characters in this story are based on real people. Molly, Arabella, Christy, and the Bells are fictional. The things that happen to them are things that could and did happen to real people in England and New York in the 1730s.

Under England's Bloody Code, more than two hundred crimes were punishable by death. Most of these crimes, such as picking pockets, were committed by poor people against rich people. Because there were more people than there was work for them to do, a large part of the population, including many children, had no way to live except by stealing. And so they stole until they were either hanged or transported to the Colonies.

They were a whole class of people who expected to

die on the gallows. Ballads and songs written at the time depict these people as mischievous, happy-go-lucky, and carefree. But the songs were certainly not written by the illiterate criminals themselves, and the real story of their lives was probably rather grim.

Every scene in the story is described as historians say it looked (and smelled). The Hold, the lowest cell in Newgate prison, really had a floor several inches deep in dead bugs. Trials at the Old Bailey court were held outside, even in the winter, and some convicts were branded with hot irons right in the court.

About fifty thousand English criminals came to the American colonies as unwilling immigrants. (That's almost five hundred times the number of passengers on the *Mayflower.*) Some of the convicts were children, and some were Jewish, like Molly.

Some English convict ships were probably as deadly as slave ships. Although nobody knows the exact numbers, it's estimated that starvation and disease killed as many as 30 percent of the convicts on the ships.

Jews in the colonies made a special effort to buy any Jewish convicts who arrived, but they didn't buy them to set them free. They bought these convicts to protect them from having to break the Jewish dietary and Sabbath laws. Eighteenth-century people didn't think of freedom the way we do now. Hardly anybody was really "free" as we use the term today. Most people lived somewhat under the control of somebody else—a master, a parent, a husband—all their lives.

In the eighteenth century, "family" meant everybody that lived in a house, whether related or not, so Mr. Bell isn't saying anything unusual when he says that his servants are members of his family. Middle-class people didn't think of their servants as social inferiors, as they would a century later. But they didn't question their right to own people either.

In the 1730s, New York City was a small town of about eight thousand people. About twelve hundred were black, most of them slaves. There had been a slave rebellion in 1712, and many New Yorkers lived in constant fear of another one. Some people mistrusted slaves who could read and Elias Neau, the Christian missionary who taught them. But it was never illegal to teach slaves to read in New York, as it was later in other states. New York did not abolish slavery until 1827.

Cows and pigs roamed freely in the streets of New York City. Most of Manhattan island was still farmland, and about one-quarter of the city's men were sailors. The people of New York came from many different countries—as they do today—and spoke mainly Dutch, English, and French.

By 1730, about 225 Jews lived in New York City. They were about equally divided between the Ashkenazic (Yiddish-speaking) and Sephardic (Ladino/Spanish/

Portuguese-speaking) groups. The synagogue in the story, Shearith Israel, was (and still is) Sephardic, but it was the only synagogue in New York until 1825, and so both groups attended. The building stood on what is now South William Street in Lower Manhattan until 1818. Shearith Israel's present synagogue is located on Central Park West. The rimonim that Molly planned to steal are still used there once a year to commemorate the founding of the synagogue on Mill Street in 1730.

Useful Flash-cant Words and Phrases

Adam-tiler: An accomplice to whom a pickpocket immediately hands what she steals so that the pickpocket will be empty-handed if caught.

autem: A church. When used in combination, anything having to do with religion: hence, "autem-ken," a church; "autem-mort," one's legally married wife or a religious woman; "autem-cove," one's legal husband or a religious man.

bene: Good; thus "to cut bene widdes," to speak kindly; "to cut bene," to be kind.

blood money: In Flash, "blood money" referred to the forty-pound monetary reward offered in England to anybody who turned in a criminal, if the criminal was subsequently hanged.

blow the gab: To turn someone in to the authorities (also "to shop," "to squeak," "to whiddle," "to cackle").

blunt: Money (also "danby," "rhino," "redge," "ginglers").

bob-: A combining form meaning "fancy."

bolt-hole: A hidden escape route.

boman: A boyfriend.

bowzy: Drunk.

bulker: An accomplice who bumps into a pickpocket's targets, distracting them while the pickpocket picks.

canting lay: Criminal activity; to be "on the canting lay" is to be a criminal.

-cheat: A combining form meaning a thing that performs or serves the purpose of. A duck is a "quacking-cheat"; clothes are "scowring (wearing)-cheats"; the "nubbing-cheat" is the gallows.

chiff, chive: A knife.

clove: A person on the canting lay.

cly: A pocket.

cove: A man or boy.

cull: A man or boy; also, a victim. A fencing cull is a person who buys stolen goods.

Deadly Nevergreen Tree: The gallows; also called "the nubbing-cheat."

dew-beater: A foot.

done over: Hanged.

downy: Knowing; streetwise.

dubber: A lock picker.

fambles: Hands.

figging lay: The pocket-picking business.

file the cly: To pick a pocket.

Flash: 1. Underworld lingo (short for "Flash-cant").
2. Anything having to do with crime: hence, "flash-cove," a criminal; "flash-ken," a thieves' den.

flat: A victim; a fool.

frummagem: To strangle.

glim: A candle; a light.

grunter: A shilling.

hempen fever: Hanging. Rope was made of hemp; thus "to have a case of hempen fever" or "to die of hempen fever" was to be hanged.

Jack Ketch: The actual name of a London hangman; by extension, any hangman.

jarkman: A forger (that is, anybody on the canting lay who could read and write).

jug-bit: Drunk.

-ken: A combining form meaning a house or building: hence, "flash-ken," a thieves' den; "bob-ken," a fancy house; "autem-ken," a religious house (a church or, by extension, a synagogue).

kinchin: A child. A word often used in combination: a "kinchin cove," a boy; a "kinchin mort," a girl.

lig: A bed.

maunderer: A beggar.

mish: A shirt or shift (underdress).

mort: A woman or girl.

nap: To catch.

nib: Fancy; well-off (at least compared to people on the canting lay). Thus "nib cull," a rich person and therefore a potential victim.

ride a horse foaled by an acorn: To be hanged (also "to be scragged," "to swing," "to be turned off").

ride the three-legged mare: To be hanged at the triple gallows at Tyburn, on the outskirts of London.

scowring-cheats: Clothes.

shop: To tell on someone; to give someone up to the authorities.

sing out beef: To cry "Stop, thief!"

snabble: To catch; to arrest.

speak with: To steal.

stalling-ken: A place where stolen goods are bought.

stamper cases: Shoes.

stook-hauler: A pickpocket who specializes in hand-kerchiefs.

stow your glim: Knock your lights out.

stow your widdes: "Shut up!"

surtoute: To know.

Tyburn Tree: The gallows at the edge of London, not actually a tree but a three-legged triangular structure joined by three crossbeams (thus "to dance the Tyburn hornpipe"—to be hanged at Tyburn).

upright-man: The leader of a gang of thieves.

whiddle: To speak; also, to tell on someone.

Acknowledgments

I would like to thank everyone who helped me in researching, fact-checking, and completing *A Pickpocket's Tale*, including Rachel Ostrow, Gregory Hays, Deborah Schwabach, Aaron Schwabach, Jennifer Schwabach, and Jon Schwabach; the staff and librarians at the Consortium Library, University of Alaska–Anchorage, and at Gramley Library, Salem College, including Donna Melton, Rose A. Simon, and the late Susan Taylor; Alana Shultz and Rabbi Marc Angel at Congregation Shearith Israel in New York City; Rachel Glasser, Sandy Gottesman Breger, Aileen Grossberg, Susan Pankowsky, Marion Stein, and Barbara Sutton of the Association of Jewish Libraries, as well as the Sydney Taylor family for their encouragement of new writers; Pamela S. Nadell, Director of the Jewish Studies Program at American University, for fact-checking; and my editor, Lisa Findlay, for everything. Any errors that remain are my own.

About the Author

Karen Schwabach grew up in upstate New York and lived for many years in Alaska, where she taught English as a Second Language in the Yup'ik Inuit village of Chefornak. She now trains ESL teachers in North Carolina. *A Pickpocket's Tale* is her first novel.